SECRETS AND SNOWFLAKES

Related titles by S. Usher Evans

PRINCESS VIGILANTE
The City of Veils
The Veil of Ashes
The Veil of Trust
The Queen of Veils

THE SEOD CROÍ CHRONICLES
A Quest of Blood and Stone
A Quest of Earth and Magic
A Quest of Sea and Soil
A Quest of Aether and Dust

THE MADION WAR TRILOGY
The Island
The Chasm
The Union

SECRETS AND SNOWFLAKES

Weary Dragon Inn

BOOK THREE

S. Usher Evans

Sun's Golden Ray
Publishing

Pensacola, FL

Version Date: 7/31/23

© 2023 S. Usher Evans

ISBN: 978-1945438660

Map created by Luke Beaber of Stardust Book Services

Line Editing by Danielle Fine, By Definition Editing

Sun's Golden Ray Publishing

Pensacola, FL

www.sgr-pub.com

For ordering information, please visit

www.sgr-pub.com/orders

Dedication

To the Kickstarter Backers

CHAPTER ONE

"Looks like snow," Vellora Witzel said.

Bev squinted at the dark sky above, a frigid, damp breeze billowing her pants as she stood in the yard behind the butcher shop. "Pretty early for it."

Although Vellora's tall, muscular torso was wrapped in three large sweaters, the butcher still didn't look comfortable. "I hate this time of year. I don't do well in the cold. Give me warm, sunny skies over this slop any day."

"Well, if we're in luck, it'll hold off until the solstice," Bev replied optimistically. "Lots of folks on the road this time of year. Would hate for them to get stuck in it."

"Too true," Vellora said, nodding to the Weary Dragon Inn in the distance. "Packed house at the inn?"

"Well, it was last night, but everyone cleared out first thing this morning," Bev said. "Already this morning, a sweet, young couple with three kids under five stopped in, as well as a nice gentleman who's traveling south."

"Three under five?" Vellora shuddered. "And traveling?"

"I haven't had a chance to chat with them much, but they seem nice enough," Bev said. "I thought the kids might like some beef stew tonight with all this cold weather. Making a couple loaves of rosemary bread, too."

Vellora's face brightened. "Your plant's growing that well?"

Bev nodded with a proud smile. "By leaps and bounds. Gotten so much off it lately, and it's nearly outgrowing the pot. If it wasn't so darn cold, I'd transplant it back into the garden. But I don't want to risk *anything* happening to it."

Vellora nodded knowingly. A few weeks ago, during the annual Pigsend Harvest Festival, Bev's prized herb garden had been ransacked by a man in search of powerful magical beings, with her beloved rosemary plant—the key ingredient to her famous bread—totally eaten by a magical-detection creature. But Ida, Vellora's wife, had come to the rescue, having snipped off a few pieces for her and her wife to enjoy—and one of those had taken root and thrived under Bev's watchful eye in a pot in her windowsill.

"So whadd'ya think? Four pounds of beef will do?" Vellora asked.

"Let's make it six," Bev said. "No telling who might show up tonight, and the last thing I want is to have an inn full of hungry travelers without enough to feed them all."

"No arguments there," Vellora said.

"Oh, before I forget," Bev said. "Can you ask Ida if she'd like to help me pick out a tree? I know she has opinions—"

"Too many," Vellora said with a loving chuckle. "She's out doing deliveries right now, but when she gets back, I'll let her know." She shivered. "Now let me get back inside before my fingers freeze off. Can't be wielding a knife if I don't have digits, you know."

⁓

The warm fire of the Weary Dragon Inn was welcoming. Bev wasn't nearly as...well, *wimpy* as Vellora when it came to the cold, but with the dreary weather outside, it was nice to be indoors. She plucked off her heavy cloak and hung it by the door, the faint smell of rosemary and rising bread permeating the kitchen. The hearth crackled with a nice-sized fire, but someone was missing from his perch in front of it.

Bev crossed the kitchen to poke her head out to the front room, listening for the sound of snoring. When she didn't hear any, she called, "Biscuit?"

Her mischievous dog (though technically another magical-detection creature called a laelaps, she'd taken to calling him a dog for ease of explanation) wasn't there either. He was about as fond of the cold as Vellora, so she doubted she'd find him in the back yard bothering Bev's faithful mule Sin (short for Sinister) or the beautiful, large horse that had pulled the family of five's wagon.

Bev hustled up the stairs; if she didn't find the dog quickly, he'd probably destroy something important. She knocked on the first closed door. "Mr. Shaffer? Sorry to interrupt—"

The door opened, revealing the solo traveler who'd checked in an hour before, Bernie Shaffer. He was pale with straw-colored hair, on the shorter side, with a round face and easygoing smile.

"Bev, what can I do for you?" he said.

"I'm so sorry," Bev said with a smile. "But have you seen my dog floating about? He's prone to trouble, and—"

"I *believe* those rascals down the hall kidnapped him," he said with a small wink. "They might've lured him with some dried beef."

"Oh, thank you," Bev said, clasping her hands together as she turned to walk down the hall. "Appreciate it!"

"Not a problem!" He waved before closing the door behind him.

Bev hurried down the hall, unsure how Mr. Biscuit would do with small children. But as she approached the other closed door, a child giggled, and she relaxed a bit.

"Excuse me?" Bev knocked on the door. "Mr. and Ms. Werst—"

"Bev, hello!" Abigail Werst opened the door, a slight whip of a woman with dark brown silky hair and medium-brown skin, who seemed happy despite the near-constant chaos at her feet. A sleeping baby girl with a crop of dark hair was wrapped to her torso. Her husband—a tall, pale man who was nearly too long for the bed he was lying in—was watching the two boys, the younger with light brown hair and the older sharing his mother and sister's dark hair and features. The two boys were hunched over something Bev couldn't see but could only guess at based on the *thump-thump-thump* of a tail on the ground.

"I was looking for—"

At the sound of her voice, Biscuit popped his head up and met Bev's gaze. He was light brown all over, save his white belly and a few spots on his feet. His eyes were a vivid gold, typical for laelaps, and his floppy ears were like velvet—perhaps why the older boy, Peter, was rubbing them so intensely.

"Oh, he's the sweetest boy," the four-year-old said.

"When he wants to be," Bev said dryly. "I wanted to make sure he wasn't causing you guys any problems."

"Are you kidding?" Abigail Werst barked out a laugh. "It's the first time these two haven't been driving us all crazy since we left home this morning. If you're fine with him staying—"

"It sounds mutually beneficial," Bev said. "You said you left this morning? Where from?"

"Oh, Gilramore," Abigail said. "West of here. We're visiting my parents in Wimborne for the first time. Thought we could make it to Middleburg, at least, but with the baby and how cold it was today, it wasn't feasible."

"Understandable," Bev said. "Glad you guys are here. I'm making beef stew for dinner, and some of my famous rosemary bread, so we'll be sure to fill you up before you head out in the morning."

Abigail beamed. "I hope the boys aren't disturbing your other guests. Let me know if they are."

"So far, it's just you and Mr. Shaffer down the

hall," Bev said. "Though I do expect more stragglers. Please, make yourselves at home and let me know if you need anything at all." She leaned over to catch Biscuit's gaze. "And you behave yourself, understand?"

The dog unfurled his tongue in a smile.

With Biscuit entertained, Bev returned to the kitchen to continue work on her bread. She added another log to the fire and went to check on the large ball of dough rising nearby. Rosemary and yeast filled her nose, and the dough had clearly doubled in size, so it was ready for the next step.

The week before the solstice marked an unusual uptick in activity for the winter months. Since the Harvest Festival had concluded the previous month, the inn had been all but deserted. But within the past three days, Bev had been booked solid, to the point where she'd been having to turn away weary travelers looking for a warm bed for the night. Typically, the trend continued until the week after the solstice, too, after which things would quiet down until the last of the snowy months ended and people started traveling again.

There was something comforting about having a rhythm to the day, the season, the year. Especially after all the chaos with the sinkholes and Harvest Festival mishaps, it had been nice to slow down and enjoy her work as innkeeper. She'd tried a few new recipes out on her usual customers, including a tweak to her rosemary bread that required an additional round of kneading as well as an update to her brewing methods. All had been well-received, not that Bev was angling to add to her Harvest Festival runner-up ribbon.

Her rosemary plant sat in the window, sucking in whatever sunlight it could from the gloomy day outside. From the small sprig, it had blossomed into a plant nearly three feet tall, with a multitude of branches. It was already in the largest pot that could sit on the sill, and it probably wasn't big enough. That it had flourished so quickly was a miracle...

Or magic.

The night after the Harvest Festival concluded, Bev had awoken to a strange amulet piece glowing in her dresser. That amulet had, up until two months ago, been buried in her garden out back, and Bev had a sense in the back of her mind it was quite powerful.

Now, Bev had moved that amulet far from the inn (and more importantly, her garden), but in doing so had uncovered *another* piece. And when she'd held the two, she'd had a vision of a horrible battle and her own hands covered in blood.

"We're ignoring that," Bev muttered to herself as she kneaded the dough.

When Bev had arrived in town five years before, she hadn't had a clue who she was. Not even her own name. But since these *little events* had started happening, more pieces of her past seemed to be coming to light, and not in a good way. If Bev wanted to spend time thinking about it, she might come to the conclusion she was somehow a part of the bloody war between the kingside and queenside that had happened years ago, and perhaps her memory loss was a result of that.

But she didn't want to spend time thinking about it. Not when there was so much to do around the inn.

"Hello? Anyone here?"

A voice echoed from the front room—a new guest. Bev sighed, looking down at her dough-covered hands. They always seemed to come in when she was working on her bread.

"Be right out!" Bev called. "Have a seat next to the fire and warm up."

She hastily finished her knead and put the dough back in the proofing basket. Then she washed her hands in the frigid water, wiping them on her apron as she came out into the front hall to greet her new guests.

An older couple, the shorter of the two men wearing a frock signifying him as a member of the clergy, were waiting beyond the front desk. The cleric had a nice, casual air about him as he pulled his cap off to reveal a black, bald head. On his left hand was a beautiful, probably expensive ruby ring. His husband seemed a bit more uptight, with clay-colored skin and gray hair coiled in locks. Though perhaps he was just cold; he couldn't stop shivering.

"Good afternoon. Are you the proprietor?" the husband asked, his teeth almost chattering.

"Yes, my name is Bev," she said, grabbing her large guestbook to add their names. "Will you be needing a room with us tonight?"

"Please," he said with a shudder. "It's freezing out there!"

"Has it started to snow?" Bev asked.

"Not yet," the cleric said. "Earth willing, it will hold off until the solstice."

Bev smiled. Not that many people out in the rural country practiced one of the few religions, but she did get traveling clergy every so often—especially around the solstice, when members would be paid to bless the food at the homes of the rich and well-connected.

"I hope so, too," Bev said. "What name should I put down for you?"

"Cordell," the cleric said. "I'm Wallace, and that's my husband Paul."

Bev wrote their names on the next empty line in the book. "We're happy to have you here, Misters

Cordell. Dinner should be ready around six in the evening. It's beef stew tonight, along with some rosemary bread and ale—"

"Complimentary, I hope?" Paul asked.

Bev nodded. The *other* thing Bev had learned about the clergy over the years was they were *incredibly* stingy, owing to their small stipend from their church. "Of course. As much as you can stomach. That'll be one gold per night."

"And without the dinner, it would be—"

"Paul," Wallace chided gently as he twisted the ring on his pinky. "Pay her the coin. It's worth it for a warm bed tonight."

Paul made a face and pulled a single gold coin from his pouch, handing it to Bev. She took it without complaint and deposited it in the small pouch she kept under the front desk.

"I've got to get back to making dinner, so please make yourselves at home. You'll be in room three."

"Thank you for the hospitality," Wallace said with a bright smile. "Your inn is very lovely."

"I take it you've never been to Pigsend before?" Bev asked. "Where are you from?"

"We hail from Farnworth, east of here," Wallace said. "Performing a blessing at the Kaiser Tuckey solstice event."

"Kaiser Tuckey?" a new voice called as a cold shot of air blew through the front door. It closed behind him, revealing a man carrying a lute and small bag around his person. His long brown hair was braided down his back and there was haphazard stubble on his neck. "What a coincidence. I've been hired to entertain there!"

"Well, isn't that a coincidence?" Wallace said. "Perhaps we can take the final leg together."

Paul's expression darkened, and Bev could practically hear him complaining about traveling with an unwashed musician.

"Let me get you checked in," Bev said. "What name should I put down for you?"

"Collin Rossiter," he said, reaching into his pocket. "I…uh…should probably ask how much before you do."

"One gold coin per night," Bev said. "Includes dinner."

He brightened. "Excellent. I usually make my year's income from these solstice events, and times are getting a little lean, you know." He handed her the coin and smiled.

"Room four for you, Mr. Rossiter," Bev said. "I will warn you there's a family with small children in room six, but they seem pleasant enough."

"I love kids." Collin grinned. "And I'd be happy to play some music for everyone this evening."

Paul muttered something under his breath, but Wallace clapped. "I love music! What a wonderful night it will be." He looked around. "But I don't see many solstice decorations. Not even a tree."

"Off to get one this afternoon." Bev glanced at the time. Ida would be popping in any moment. "Goodness me, I've got to get dinner sorted before I leave." She paused, not wanting to ask Paul...but Wallace and Collin would be up for it. "I do hate to ask, but if either of you would keep an ear out for anyone else coming in and let them know I'll be back within an hour or so?"

Paul clicked his tongue, but Collin nodded. "Of course! I need to tune my lute anyway, so I'd be happy to sit down here and wait."

"Excellent. Much appreciated." She smiled as the back door opened. "I'll be back as soon as I can."

Chapter Two

"I hear you need my *brilliant* expertise in finding a tree," Ida said, as she walked into the kitchen dramatically carrying Bev's six pounds of beef. "Because you *obviously* can't be trusted on your own."

Bev had to smile. Where Vellora was pale, tall, and muscular, her wife was petite and lithe with tawny skin and black corkscrew hair that hung around her cheekbones today. She wore a purple sweater over her usual tunic, along with tall leather boots ready for adventure.

"Well, considering the amount of gold you're paying to rent out the inn for the solstice, I'd better make sure it's perfect, hadn't I?" Bev replied.

"Oh, speaking of gold." Ida pulled a large satchel from her hip. "For you, madam."

Bev took the satchel, not bothering to count it. "Are you sure? I don't mind hosting you for free—"

"No, Bev." Ida closed Bev's fingers around the satchel. "I insist. You're already giving us a huge discount. Wim used to charge my parents twice this amount."

Bev couldn't argue, so she hid the satchel in her cabinet, planning on saving it for a rainy day. "Let me get this in the oven, and we can leave."

Ida leaned on the kitchen table as Bev prepared the stew meat, adding herbs, a bit of red wine, and a little butter. "I'm so excited. It's been at least a decade since we've had it anywhere other than the shop, and let's say it's not...well, it's not *festive* to have thirty farmers crammed into such a small space."

Bev had briefly attended the party last year and quickly seen herself out, as there was barely room for anyone to stand.

"Well, you know I'm happy to do it," Bev said. "But I do want to make sure everything's to your exact specifications."

"Don't lie, Bev. You want me to carry the tree back."

Bev lifted a shoulder. "You caught me."

Ida smiled. Even though she was a quarter the size of her wife, she could lift three times her weight —a byproduct of her magical lineage. Exactly where that lineage came from, Bev hadn't a clue, nor had Ida done any investigating. It remained something of an untouched secret, even in the quiet weeks since the Harvest Festival.

"We need to hurry, though," Bev said, glancing at the clock. "Sun will be down soon, and I'm sure the rest of the rooms will fill up. Do you have an idea where you want to find one?"

Ida scoffed. "C'mon, Bev. It's me. Of course I do."

There were a few places to find a suitable solstice tree, especially if one listened to Ida. She'd grown up in this town, as had several generations of her family, and seemed to know every inch of the land around Pigsend village. She, unlike her wife, was unbothered by the cold, marching toward a small patch of trees with a determined yet joyful look on her face.

"When I was a little girl, my grandfather brought me here every winter to chop down a tree," she said, an old axe resting on her shoulders as she walked. "This axe has been used for every Witzel solstice tree the last hundred years at least."

"What are we looking for?" Bev asked.

"Well, a *true* solstice tree is going to be a spruce or fir, of course. There's a small grove where they grow pretty quickly. Seems like there's always a bunch of them, no matter how many get chopped down."

They were along the path of the underground magical river she'd discovered a few months ago. "The front room of the inn is pretty tall, so we can find a big one."

"I plan on it," Ida said. "I'm so glad we're able to afford the inn again. It hasn't been the same since my folks died."

"How did they—"

"Dragon pox, about seven years ago." She shook her head. "Just a shame they never met Vellora. They would've *loved* her."

"Do you have any other family around?" Bev asked. She hadn't seen any, which was odd, considering Ida's deep roots in town.

"Oh, here and there. No one worth mentioning, though. There was a large schism in the Witzel family when my great-grandfather took the butchery over. His brother was a scoundrel, nearly ran it into the ground. But it was supposed to be split between the two of them, and the brother's side of the family hasn't ever forgiven mine for 'stealing' the butcher business from them."

Bev wasn't asking for conversation's sake. "Any

luck finding out where this...strength comes from? The dryad?"

Ida tripped over her feet, turning to Bev with a sideways look. "Kind of. Since things have been a little quiet, Vel's asked me to spend some time in the library, poring over family trees to try to find a clue. But it's boring work, and I haven't found much I didn't already know. Just names of ancestors and no notes about anything special."

Bev nodded. While Ida's strength hadn't been much of a secret, the source of it had been revealed during the Harvest Festival. *Maybe.* Claude (or Renault as he was actually called) had speculated she was a dryad. Although Bev had never heard the term, she'd found out it was a woodland nymph from her encyclopedia of magical creatures.

"Well, that's why I was asking about other family," Bev said. "They might know something?"

"There's been no one like me in town since... well, ever," Ida said. "At least no one worth talking about. And Vel's skittish about me asking too many questions of the townsfolk. She doesn't want the wrong person to find out about me and turn me in."

"To whom?" Bev asked. "There hasn't been a queen's soldier in town for weeks."

"Yeah, but they keep coming through, and you know my wife. Paranoid as all get out." She laughed, but there was a little sadness there. "You know, she won't even tell me about *her* family or where she's from. Too nervous it's going to come back to bite her. I know it was somewhere south. But I would love to meet her family someday."

Bev slowed. "You really don't know *anything* about your wife?"

"I mean, I know *her*," Ida said. "I love *her*. But the details…" She sighed. "She still gets nightmares from her time in the war. I want to know, but I also don't want to press if she's… There's a lot of trauma there I can't even begin to understand." She glanced at Bev. "We can't all have lost our memories and live in blissful ignorance."

Bev let out a small chuckle. "What can I say? I got the luck of the draw on that one."

They reached the grove, and as Ida had said, it was filled with all sizes of coniferous trees, some of which appeared too tall for even the Weary Dragon Inn's large front room.

"Well, how about that one?" Bev said, pointing to a nearby one.

"Bev, seriously?" Ida made a noise. "You have to *really look* at them. It's not an easy decision."

And look she did, pacing around each tree, pulling at the limb and deciding if they were sturdy enough for the decorations she was planning to add to them.

"Yes, see this one is a fine height, but I'm not

sure about the *girth*," Ida muttered. "The shape is off. But if we turn it so only *this* side is visible."

Bev glanced at the sky, which was growing darker—and not from snow. "I do need to be getting back. I typically get an influx of people when the sun sets."

"Fine." Ida took three steps back and chewed her lip. "That one. It's not *exactly* what I'm looking for, but—"

"It'll do."

Bev turned out to be quite superfluous, as Ida insisted on chopping the tree herself to make sure it was a perfect cut. Then, of course, the super-strong woman carried the tree back into town on her shoulder as if it weighed absolutely nothing. Bev carried the axe, making sure to keep it off the ground. It was heavy, but perhaps not as heavy as the tree.

"So, expecting another busy night?" Ida said.

"Indeed," Bev said. "We got a cleric and his husband, and a traveling bard before I left. Two rooms empty now."

"Oh, well, it's a shame they can't stay for the solstice. That would be fortuitous." Ida snorted. "Not that we can afford such things."

Bev nodded. "I hear they're going to Kaiser Tuckey's place. He lives near Middleburg, right?"

"Yeah. Richest man in the area, for sure. Don't know why his ancestor picked all the way out here to build his mansion, but he did and they've lived here ever since." She tilted her head. "I went there once, you know. He opens his manor in the spring for the locals to tour. Wants them to get some *culture*." She paused. "You know Ramone used to work for him, right?"

"No, I didn't." The nonbinary sculptor had moved to town three years ago, but Bev had thought they worked in Queen's Capital. "I wonder when they'll be done with the dragon fountain? The town square isn't quite the same without it." It had been one of the casualties of the sinkholes that had plagued the town.

"I'm sure they'll have it ready by spring. Who knows? It might be ready now, and they just don't want to drag it all the way into town." She snorted. "I wouldn't be surprised if I get asked to move it."

"Well, considering…" Bev gestured to the tree. "It might be easier for you."

She lifted a shoulder as the Weary Dragon Inn came into view. "So, where should I put this?"

"I'll leave that up to you," Bev said. "I was hoping to get out to Herman Monday's house. He's paid me ten gold pieces to check on his goats while he's traveling for the solstice."

"Just making all the money, aren't you?" Ida said

29

with a chuckle. "Hoping to retire early or something?"

"Nah. Just being helpful," Bev said as they came to a fork in the road. "I'll leave the tree placement in your very capable hands. If anyone's waiting, let them know I should be back soon to check them in."

~

Herman's house was fine, and Bev added extra feed to the goats' troughs and pumped more water for them. They were unimpressed with her efforts. She did a quick check of his house to ensure everything was secure before heading back to town. It wasn't even four in the afternoon, but the sky was already growing darker—it was the shortest day of the year after all—and she wanted to be back at the inn to intercept any last stragglers.

There was, fortunately, only one person waiting to check in when Bev returned—a lovely young woman with freckled skin, wavy auburn hair, and a timid expression.

"Estera Pongo," she said. "Just one night. Appreciate it. The last three inns I tried were booked solid."

"Of course," Bev said, writing her name down. "Where are you coming from?"

"Oh, um. Just north of here." Her pale cheeks flushed. "Anyway. I'm glad you had space."

"I've got one left, if you've got any friends," Bev said, handing her the key. "Room two."

Bev propped the kitchen door open as she set about finishing the preparations for dinner. The bread was perfect and ready for the oven, and Bev even scored a few designs on the top, for festivity's sake. The beef was cooking well, with the smell permeating the kitchen every time she opened the lid to check on it.

The smell, of course, drew Biscuit into the kitchen. He walked with his light brown nose pointed in the air, his tail wagging as he stretched his little body as long as it could go in search of goodies on the kitchen table. Unfortunately, he hadn't come alone, as the two mischievous boys followed him.

"I'm *hungry*," the oldest whined. "Is it ready yet?"

"Not quite," Bev said with a kind smile. "But I think I've got some dried meat in that cabinet over there if you'll go look."

It was, of course, a terrible idea as the three pulled everything out of the cabinet in search of the promised dried meat. Bev let them destroy the cabinet—it was one cabinet instead of the entire inn—they were eventually rewarded with a piece of dried beef apiece. Even Biscuit.

"Now head out into the dining room," Bev said.

"I'll be out with dinner shortly."

Dinner was lively, as it had been with a completely full inn the past few days. Bev's usual customers—Earl Dollman, the carpenter, and Etheldra Daws, owner of the tea shop—showed up to eat, as did Max Sterling, the librarian. The two little boys ate quickly and ran around playing tag, while Collin the bard struck up a jaunty tune that had the entire room clapping along. Even the little baby girl seemed in a great mood, giggling and waving her arms in her father's lap.

"Oh, that was fun!" Collin said, grabbing a sip of ale. "Any other requests?"

"Let's have a solstice tune," Wallace said, toying with his ring. "Do you know *As The Weather Turns*?"

"Do I? It's one of my favorites," Collin said, pulling his lute back into position. His fingers moved along the strings expertly, weaving a somewhat familiar and pleasing melody.

The days are darker
The nights are colder
The air is unwelcoming
But here at the hearth, all is well

Come to the fire
Drink with me to your health
And let's celebrate the coming light
As the weather turns brighter

At solstice's end

"Again! Again!" Wallace said, his eyes misty from the three tankards of ale he'd imbibed. Beside him, Paul looked a bit uncomfortable, nudging him and whispering in his ear.

The bard struck up the tune once more, and the two little boys grabbed each other's hands, spinning around the room. Too late, Bev called out for them to stop, as they crashed into the wall, knocking over a vase that shattered on the floor.

"Oh goodness, Bev," Abigail said, running to Bev while Byron tended to the boys. "I'm so sorry. Please let me know how much that cost, and I'd be happy to replace it."

"Don't you mind," Bev said. "It was a gift from the local sculptor. And when I say gift, it was one of their castoffs they didn't want to see again. Anyway, that's hardly the first sculpture that's been broken in this room…"

Abigail's face relaxed. "You've got the patience of a saint, Bev."

"You lot are far more enjoyable than some of the patrons I've had here," Bev said. "I once had a quintet of queen's soldiers."

Her expression faltered, and Bev realized too late she perhaps should've qualified her statement.

"They weren't the nicest," Bev said. "But I've nothing against them as a general rule. As long as they don't cause the front of my inn to fall into a sinkhole, I've got no quarrel."

Abigail forced a smile onto her face. "I think that's reasonable. Let me go tend to my hellions. But I insist." She placed a gold coin on the table. "For all you've done to put up with us today."

Bev pushed it back to her. "Save it. I'm sure you'll need it on your journey."

"Shall I do another tune?" Collin asked as the murmuring of the room began again. "Something a bit slower?"

"Please," Paul said with a moan as he rubbed his head.

"How about *Here We Go into the Dark*?" Wallace said. "That's rather slow."

Collin adjusted his lute. "I think I remember that one. Let's see…"

He strummed the first line and had opened his mouth to sing when the front door burst open. A figure cloaked in black walked inside, the only thing visible were his dark eyes. He walked straight up to Bev and, without removing his wrappings, demanded to know how much a night was.

"Uh, one gold," Bev said, a little taken aback by the brusqueness. "And you're in luck, because it's the last—"

He slammed down one gold coin and held out his hand. "Key."

"What name should I put down for you?" Bev asked, picking up her quill and dipping it in the ink.

"Why do you need to know?" he snapped.

"I like to keep a log of all my guests," Bev said. "Makes it easier to remember who's who."

"I'm leaving at first light." He shifted. "You can put down H."

"H. That works for me." Bev wrote down the letter. "Here you go." Bev handed him her last remaining key. "Number five—"

She barely got the word out before he walked toward the staircase and disappeared.

The entire room stared at each other, unsure what to say after such an arrival.

Bev loudly cleared her throat and forced a smile. "Let's have that tune, Collin," she said. "After all, we're all here for one night. Might as well enjoy it!"

CHAPTER THREE

When Bev awoke the next morning, there was a chill in the air. She walked by the window, stopped, then turned to get a closer look.

It was still dark, but it appeared there was a thick blanket of snow over…well, everything. Bev dressed and put on a warm sweater and her trusty boots as she quietly descended the stairs, Biscuit sleepily at her heels. Downstairs was frigid as well, as the fires from the night before had long since gone out. She worked quickly to light the kindling, and just as soon as the flames were high enough to give off heat, Biscuit curled into a ball and fell asleep in front of it.

"You keep sleeping." Bev shook her head. "I'll do all the work."

She walked to the front door, pulling it open to see how much snow had actually fallen. Her brows rose as she gazed out at the still-dark road. Six inches, at least, and based on the fluffy flakes falling from the sky currently, there would be more to come.

"Well, I'll be," Bev muttered, closing the door to keep the chill out.

It wasn't unheard of to get snow before the solstice in Pigsend, but it certainly made things more difficult for her traveling guests. She hoped, for their sake, the snow ended quickly and the day warmed up.

She made a second fire in the kitchen and set to her daily chores, checking on Sin and the Wersts' horse and giving them some hay and oats. Even the walk from the kitchen to the stables was difficult with the high snow, and Bev couldn't imagine trying to get back out on the road in these conditions.

With that in mind, and knowing that those parents especially could use a pick-me-up, she doubled her usual batch of bread dough, intending to set some aside for cinnamon rolls for later that day. She had more cinnamon sticks on hand to make her traditional solstice wassail, made with ale, cinnamon, and cloves, but she could spare a tablespoon. She usually left the sweets to Allen Mackey, the local baker whose shop was next door, but it was hard to resist a cinnamon roll made with her bread dough.

The dark sky didn't brighten much as the sun came up, and the snow hadn't stopped either. Her guests were moving about upstairs, and she hated to think how each of them would react to being stuck in Pigsend. The smell of yeast and bread dough woke Biscuit, and he pushed the kitchen door open to sit next to the fire, yawning loudly.

"You're awfully lazy today," Bev said. "Did those kids wear you out yesterday.?"

He stretched out by the fire and fell asleep.

"Guess that answers that," Bev said.

Someone was walking down the stairs, so Bev wiped her hands on her apron to greet them. Allen hadn't been by with his basket of breakfast pastries yet, but she could at least offer the early riser a cup of tea.

Unsurprisingly, it was the Mysterious H. Bev hesitated to say good morning at all, especially since he was already dressed for the weather, but she thought it sporting to at least warn him of what he'd encounter.

"Heavy snow fell last night," she said, causing him to freeze in the middle of the room.

"What?" he said, his voice muffled by the

coverings over his face.

"I said there was a heavy snowfall last night," Bev said softer. "And it's still coming down. Might make things more difficult. You're welcome to stay and see if it'll melt off."

"No."

He turned and walked to the door, pulling it open and stopping short. Perhaps he hadn't understood what *heavy* meant, because he stood in the doorway, contemplating if the calf-deep-and-still-falling snow was worth trudging in.

Evidently, he decided it was, because he took a large step outside, closing the door behind him.

"Well, good luck to you," Bev muttered.

It was early, and she didn't hear movement upstairs yet, so she pulled a piece of blank paper from her stack beneath the counter and began brainstorming her menu for the Witzel solstice party. Ida had invited forty people, though more would probably show up. It would be a lot of food to prepare, and most of it needed to be done the day of, but there were ways to make her life a little easier.

Allen would be making the ginger cake and shortbread, and Bev was excited to taste what the baker would come up with now that he'd found his groove. Ida and Vellora would bring the solstice log, decorating it with fragrant spruce leaves to fill the front room with an earthy, festive scent. They'd be giving each of the farmers a small bag of the ashes to spread in their fields for the next year in hopes of another excellent season. They'd also provide the pork to be cooked, which would take most of the day. Wim had once put together a schedule for when he'd hosted parties for the Witzels in the past, and Bev made a mental note to go upstairs looking for it later.

The rest of the meal would be rounded out with nuts and winter berries, along with some late winter squash she'd been keeping in her salt cellar, potatoes, and lots and lots of rosemary bread.

Bev chewed her lip. The bread could *perhaps* be baked the day before, but as to the rest of it…

The front door flew open, nearly sending her off her stool. She put her hand to her heart, looking up as the Mysterious H came storming back in, his pants soaked up past the knees. He said nothing to Bev, but marched back upstairs and slammed the door.

"Well, I guess that answers that question," Bev muttered.

It seemed the Mysterious H wasn't the only one deterred by the snow. Abigail looked like she was going to cry, as did her husband, though the little boys were eager to get out and romp around in it.

Bev promised them both a cinnamon roll apiece if they'd check on the animals for her (leaving out that they'd already been tended to)—earning a relieved sigh from the weary parents.

"Thank you again," Abigail said, clasping Bev's hand. "You've got a way with kids."

"Well, it'll give Biscuit a break from them for sure."

Allen arrived with his basket of breakfast muffins, much to the joy of the little boys and their parents. Bernie, from room one, came walking down the stairs talking with Estera, from room two, and they both seemed unbothered about the snow.

"I can't say I'm mad to spend another night here, if that's the case," Bernie said, taking a muffin.

"Me either, especially if these muffins keep coming," Estera said.

Paul, the husband of the clergyman from room three, made it down before Wallace, and was very curious to know if Bev would charge them full price for another night.

"Since, well, it's not within our control that we're still here," Paul said.

"Let's cross that bridge when we get there," Bev said with a kind smile. "I'm sure we can work out something."

The sun was all the way up by the time Wallace, Paul's husband, and Collin, the bard in room four, came down. Wallace looked like those ales had really taken their toll on him, and Collin had the same question about the next night.

"Let's all see what happens," Bev said, holding up her hands. "I'm headed out to check on a house down the road, so I'll be happy to let you know what things look like. Believe me, I don't want any of you missing your engagements, but if it's not safe, it's not safe."

Even with Bev's knee-high leather boots and warm socks, it was tough to walk down the street. The Weary Dragon was one of the last buildings in the village of Pigsend, and the closest farm was a fifteen-minute walk on a good day. Today, Bev found herself huffing and puffing as her feet sank into the frigid, wet snow.

Behind her, Biscuit was struggling to keep up, leaping over the snow before disappearing into the white.

"Go home, B," Bev said, wiping her sweaty brow. "It's too cold for you to be out here like this."

But the loyal little laelaps kept behind her.

Finally, Bev had to stop and catch her breath, leaning against a fence post. Behind her, she could still see the thatched roof of the Weary Dragon. She'd perhaps gone half a mile at most.

"This might not happen today," she muttered to

Biscuit. "I feel bad, but you know, those goats are probably fine."

"Bev? Is that you?"

Bev rose from the fencepost and squinted at the house behind her. There was a tall, lanky figure on the porch, wrapped in a dramatic cloak and scarf. Ramone Comely, the local sculptor, waved. They were of average height, with thick arms and legs, perhaps from years of sculpting stone. Their curly dark brown hair, flecked with gold, was barely visible under a matching hat, and their golden skin was pale from the cold wind.

"Ramone? I really haven't made it that far, have I?" Bev asked. Ramone lived only two houses down from the inn.

"Seems a bad day to be out and about," they said, struggling to cross the distance between the two of them. "Why don't you come in for a cuppa?"

Any other day, Bev would've declined, as she needed to get back to the inn, but she was in need of a break from the difficult walk. "That would be lovely, thank you." She picked up Biscuit and trudged toward the sculptor. "What a day, eh?"

"Miserable." They sniffed. "Come, come. I've got a new blend I've been dying to try."

Ramone's artistic flair was all over their tiny little home, from the canvas paintings on the wall to the sculptures, vases, and other pottery sitting on every shelf, nook, and cranny in the place. Bev didn't want to put Biscuit down for fear he might break something.

"Sit, sit," Ramone said. "I've just put on a kettle."

Bev sat on the oddest couch she'd ever seen—it was painted with a floral pattern, with two armrests, but the back was missing.

Biscuit lifted his snout in the air and sniffed, wagging his tail.

"Don't you be looking for any magic in here," Bev muttered to him.

In the kitchen, the kettle whistled, and Ramone bustled about, getting things ready.

"So you said this is a new blend?" Bev asked.

"Yes. I buy in bulk from Etheldra's shop and like to make my own concoctions. A pinch of this, a dab of that. I've offered my blends to her, but she's only interested in the basics. Boring, if you ask me."

Bev nodded as the sculptor reappeared with two large mugs. "Did you make everything in here?"

"I did," they said proudly. "Just little things to keep my hands busy in-between the larger projects."

Bev nodded. "How's the dragon fountain coming?"

Their face darkened. "Don't ask."

"Apologies," Bev said, ducking her head. She wasn't familiar with the ins and outs of artisans, but

Ramone had always been a bit dramatic.

"It *vexes* me, the design," they said, pulling a dragon fountain miniature from beneath their chair. "I can't get a clear picture of what I want."

With a huff, they tossed the miniature behind them, and it smashed into a thousand pieces.

"Sorry to hear that," Bev said, sipping the tea. It was fruity, with a hint of dried peach and something else she couldn't put her finger on. "This is quite good, Ramone. You've got a knack for this stuff."

They beamed, playing with their hands. "I'm not good with social things, you know. But I've always liked you, Bev. You seem like good people."

"I try to be good people," she said, glancing out the window. The snow had started again. "I wish this weather would change. I've got an inn full of travelers eager to get to their destinations, and I don't think they're going anywhere tonight."

"Perhaps not," Ramone said with a sigh. "It must be fascinating, meeting all those people from everywhere."

"Sometimes," Bev said, thinking of the reclusive H. Had he decided to brave the elements again? "Actually, one of my guests knocked over the vase you gave me. Would it be possible to get another one?"

"Which one did you have?" they asked with a frown.

"Well, it had a wyvern on it, and—"

"Actually, never mind," Ramone said, waving their hands. "Let me make you a new one. I insist. It'll be a nice distraction from all this…fountain business."

"If you want," Bev said. "You know, it's funny. I have a clergyman and a bard who are both headed to Kaiser Tuckey's place. Didn't you used to—"

In a flash, Ramone yanked the mug from Bev's hand and rose with a furious look on their face. "Get out."

"I—what?" Bev blinked, confused. "What did I say?"

"You uttered that *ghastly* name in my presence. Get. Out."

"Ramone, I'm so sorry that I—"

"*Get. Out.*"

Bev stumbled back toward the Weary Dragon Inn, having to carry Biscuit through the snow. She felt positively awful for offending Ramone so carelessly, but she couldn't have known about the sordid history (whatever it might be) between the artist and their former patron.

She breathed a sigh of relief when she came closer to town, and found that a wonderful citizen had at least shoveled some of the roads to make walking a bit easier. She put Biscuit down and he shook himself, continuing to the inn. Bev had just opened the door to let him inside when something caught her gaze.

Vellora and Ida were standing in their front window, reading a folded piece of paper and looking quite distressed. Bev hesitated. She didn't want to be nosy, but something tugged at her to check on them. After all, she did need to place her order for dinner…

She knocked on the door and poked her head inside. "Everything all right?"

Vellora hid the paper, but Ida waved her hand at her wife. "Hush, Vel. Yes, Bev. Come on in. We were just…" She licked her lips. "Well, we were reading what someone thought to be a good joke, I'm sure."

"It's not a joke, Ida," Vellora said. "This sort of thing is serious."

"What is it?" Bev asked.

Vellora paused for a moment then, after another encouraging look from her wife, handed Bev the letter. "We found this strapped to a rock on our back step this morning."

> *Your secrets are no longer safe.*
> *Put 50 gold coins in a bag on your back step by nightfall or I will tell everyone what I know about you.*

CHAPTER FOUR

Bev read the letter three times, trying to make sense of it. "What secrets are they talking about?"

"Clearly, Ida's magic," Vellora said.

"Now, we don't know that, honey," Ida said, a little tersely. "It could be your past, for all we know."

"Not when you've been walking about town carrying large trees three times your size," Vellora said.

"I don't think we should jump to conclusions," Bev said, folding the letter and putting it on the counter. "Or get overly bent out of shape without good reason. If Ida is the 'secret,' then who are they planning to tell?" Bev cracked a smile. "Everyone in town knows about Ida's strength. It's honestly laughable, isn't it?"

But Bev was the only one smiling.

"Then perhaps it's someone who isn't from Pigsend," Ida said softly.

"Either way, why would they threaten us unless they had good reason?" Vellora countered. "They may know something we don't."

Bev slid the letter over to Ida. "Then you should bring this to Sheriff Rustin. Have him investigate."

Vellora snorted. "And he'll do what?"

"He's been so helpful before," Ida replied.

"Yes, but this is…well, this is very clearly an attempt at blackmail," Bev said. "Which should be in his wheelhouse as a law enforcement officer."

The two butchers stared at her dubiously.

"Fine. What are you planning to do?" Bev asked.

"Well, I figure there's a slew of new folks staying at the Weary Dragon," Vellora said, cracking her knuckles. "Might be a fine day to walk over there and threaten a few people."

"You aren't going to threaten my guests," Bev replied dryly. "Without reason, of course."

"I mean…" Ida snatched the letter from Bev and read it again, worrying her bottom lip. "Maybe it's not anything serious. Maybe someone's playing a little solstice prank on us. That's a thing, right?"

If it was, Bev had never heard of it, and based on

Vellora's eye roll, it didn't look to be.

"Look, it makes sense that it's someone over at the inn," Vellora said, taking the letter from her wife. "Ida dropped that huge solstice tree off yesterday all by herself. Maybe someone saw her and thought they might try to make some quick coin."

"Well, who could it be?" Ida asked. "Did anyone strange check into the inn yesterday?"

Bev nodded slowly. "Just one. A man who came in after dinner and refused to give his name."

Vellora straightened, seemingly ready to walk out the door and throttle the man.

"*But*," Bev said loudly, "he was very eager to leave this morning. Someone who's blackmailing the local butcher wouldn't be so keen to get on his way before he got his gold."

"Maybe he said that to throw you off," Ida said.

Bev shrugged. "If he's still there when I get back to the inn, I'll keep an eye on him. But I don't know if you two have been outside yet. The roads are practically impassable. I couldn't even make it to Herman's house. Had to turn back." She decided against mentioning her disastrous tea with Ramone.

"Well, that's perfect, isn't it? We can smoke the guilty culprit out." Vellora rubbed her hands together.

Bev thought it would've been *better* had people been able to leave, but she didn't feel like arguing with the butcher. "There's a priest and his husband. I could *possibly* see them trying to score quick coin, but they seem nice enough, and I can't imagine a cleric blackmailing anyone."

Vellora snorted. "You'd be surprised."

"Who else?" Ida asked.

"A family with three kids under five, a traveling bard—another possible suspect. Then there's Estera and Bernie. I haven't had a chance to talk with them too much." She paused. "They didn't seem too upset about the snow, to be honest. They might be a good place to start."

"So we'll go over and *ask some questions*," Vellora said with an evil grin.

"No, *you'll* stay here." Bev turned the letter over again, staring at the handwriting. "You know… Maybe I can get some handwriting samples from the guests who are still around."

"How will you do that?" Ida asked.

Bev shrugged. "Maybe… Maybe I'll break out the old guestbook Wim used to keep. He liked to have people sign their names, where they were going, and how long they planned to stay, but I found it cumbersome to keep asking people, and some folks didn't like to divulge all that information anyway. They rarely did it. But if I can find it, I'll ask each of the guests to scribble a bit in it." Another pause. "Maybe I'll say it's for posterity because of the freak pre-solstice snowstorm. I need to locate his solstice plans anyway."

Ida brightened. "That's brilliant!"

Vellora didn't look convinced. "I still say I should head over there and roll some heads. They don't know who they're messing with."

"Darling, if they wrote this note, clearly they do," Ida said with a brief smile.

"We'll get to the bottom of this," Bev said. "I promise. You won't need to pay anyone anything. And when we do find out who's responsible, I'll let you put some good ol' fashioned fear into them. Sound good?"

"Bev?"

Bev wasn't two steps out the door before Vellora met her on the shoveled street. The tall, muscular butcher seemed to have shrunk in stature as she approached, her shoulders hunched and her gaze turned to the road.

"What is it?" Bev asked.

"Look, I just…" She rubbed her hands together. "Goodness, it's cold out here."

"Go back inside," Bev said. "I told you I'll handle it."

"Yes, but…" She finally lifted her gaze to meet Bev's. "Look, I need you to understand the importance of getting this right. If someone were to take Ida away... I don't know what I'd do with myself. I have to protect my family. Even if it means packing up my wife and skipping town."

Bev let out a breath. "I don't think it'll come to that."

"You don't know," Vellora said. "I mean, we can't be sure she's a druid or whatever—"

"Dryad," Bev said. "And you're right, we can't be sure of that. But I think you're focused on the wrong thing. Who's there to tell? Everyone in Pigsend knows who Ida is. Everyone's seen her carrying hundreds of pounds of beef across town without breaking a sweat."

"Exactly," Vellora said. "So clearly, they know something we don't."

"Or they're trying to scare you into giving them money," Bev said gently. "I know you're worried, and you have every right to be, but think about this clearly. The only queen's folk in town right now are Rustin, who can barely do his job, and Mayor Hendry, whose loyalties tend to...well..." Bev motioned to the air. "They're not always so strong, depending on the wind, you know?" She glanced at the inn behind her. "So if it is someone from out of town, they probably don't realize the kind of people we have in Pigsend. We don't turn on our neighbors like that. They probably didn't account for this snowstorm, either. There's nobody coming in or out on these roads."

Vellora's shoulders loosened. "I suppose you're right. But I'd still like to know who sent it so I can...*thank* them for it."

"And as soon as I figure that out," Bev said, waving the letter, "I'll let you have a crack at them. Just try to keep your head on straight until I do, okay?"

"I don't want anything to happen to my family," Vellora whispered, shaking her head. "I love Ida with everything I have and..." She swallowed hard. "She's *all* I have, actually."

"You have me, too," Bev said, squeezing her arm, which was covered in goosebumps. "Now get back inside before you freeze to death. As soon as I have an answer, I'll let you know."

~

"How's it looking out there?" Bernie asked as Bev walked through the door.

"Is it okay for us to leave?" Paul pressed.

"Well, I'll tell you the good news and the bad news," Bev said, hanging up her cloak. "The good news is that someone's been kind enough to shovel a path through the main streets of the village. So if you'd like to get out and stretch your legs, you can do so. The bad news is that beyond the city..." She sighed. "I couldn't even make it down the road to the farmer's house."

A chorus of groans echoed from the group, and Paul and his husband began whispering together.

"So I suppose we should go ahead and pay for another night, huh?" Byron asked, reaching into his coin purse to pull another gold. "I don't think Abby's going to want to take the baby out in this weather."

"Perhaps not," Bev said, debating if she should charge full price or not. "Look, why don't we call it a silver tonight for anyone who's stuck."

Paul, Collin, and Estera looked visibly relieved, while Abigail walked up to her husband and elbowed him roughly.

"No, we insist on paying full price, especially since we have the littles," she said.

Byron seemed to want to argue, but instead slid over a gold coin.

"Well, I appreciate it," Bev said. "But it's not necessary."

The conversation ended abruptly when the boys ventured too close to the hearth and pokers, and both parents scrambled over to retrieve them. Bev took the coin and placed it in her purse, knowing it was better not to argue with guests.

"I think we'll wait to see what the weather does," Paul said, after a moment. "I'm sure the warm sun will melt some of the snow."

Bev glanced at the clock—it was already midday,

and more snow looked to be on the way. "Whatever you feel comfortable with."

"I'll stay another night," Bernie said, walking over and sliding a silver coin across the counter.

"Me too," Estera said, though she took a bit longer to locate a coin. "No use in delaying the inevitable."

"Anyone else?" Bev asked, glancing at Collin.

"I think I'll wait, too," Collin said, sheepishly. "Hope springs eternal, you know."

"Obviously there's no rush," Bev said. "I doubt anyone's going to be coming into town looking for a place to sleep tonight, so there's no danger of losing your room." She put her coin purse on her hip. "Now if you'll excuse me for a moment, I've got to…uh… I'll be right back."

Bev retrieved a broom and her trusty glowing stick—a tree branch covered with mushrooms that glowed in the dark—and headed up to the second floor, lost in thought. It would've been easy to point fingers at Estera, Bernie, and the Werst family for being eager to stay, but it was as easy to say that the clerical couple and the bard were acting coy but really meaning to stay.

She tilted her head up as she walked toward the end of the hall until she reached the square frame on the ceiling that hid the attic ladder. With the broom handle, she pushed the inside of the frame up, letting a long rope down. Bev tugged hard, pulling the attic door down, along with the attached wooden ladder—and a thick veil of dust.

"Well," she coughed, waving the air in front of her face to clear it, "at least I brought the broom."

She stuck the glowing stick in the back of her pants so she could hold on to the rickety ladder with both hands. The attic was pitch black, as predicted, and the mushrooms lit up immediately. She pulled the stick from the back of her pants and held it aloft, revealing a dust-covered space filled with boxes and crates.

"Now, where'd I put that stupid thing…"

Bev hadn't a clue what was up here—it had been filled with boxes and sealed crates since she'd arrived five years ago. She'd always promised herself one day, when things were quiet, she'd spend some time going through them and getting rid of what wasn't needed. But this place had a habit of being out of sight, out of mind until she had a reason to venture up here.

She had an inkling of where the old guestbook might've been stashed. When Wim died, Bev had gathered all his personal effects and placed them in his steamer trunk up here, mostly because she was too distraught to part with her mentor's things. She'd probably put the guestbook in there, too.

She walked the length of the attic, squinting in the dark until she saw the steamer chest. It brought back memories, as it had been at the foot of Wim's bed as long as she'd known him. She walked over, kneeling in front of it, and opened the top slowly.

She wasn't sure what she was expecting—perhaps a faint whiff of that earthy ale smell—but she was disappointed when it was more of the same musty odor. She cast the glowing stick over the steamer trunk and smiled. There were Wim's three pairs of pants, his white shirts, his well-worn boots. Some books he'd kept in his room. His favorite ale tankard. The simple things of a simple man who'd enjoyed life as it was.

Bev rubbed a bit of irritation from her eyes; must've been all the dust up here.

Wim would've been furious with her for getting so sentimental when there were chores to be done, so she rustled through the trunk in search of the guestbook. Her fingers closed around a thick, heavy leather-bound book and she smiled, pulling it out and bringing her glowing stick closer. She flipped through the dust-covered pages until she found a page bearing her own handwriting from five years ago.

Unknown

Room Six
Purpose of Visit: Unsure
Duration of Visit: Unsure
Destination: Unsure

Bev had to laugh. Those first few weeks in Pigsend were a bit of a haze, floating between meeting all manner of new people, learning how to tap the ale casks and pour the perfect pint. It wasn't until much later that she learned that there'd always been *one* person working at the Weary Dragon, which wasn't ever so busy that a beverage wench was *needed*. Wim had taken pity on a lost soul.

Bev had spent her first years in room six, until Wim died and she'd moved into the innkeeper's space. Even now, she got a pang of nostalgia walking by the door.

"Bev?" Wallace's voice echoed from the open attic door. "Are you up there? I've convinced my stingy husband it would do neither of us good to leave in this weather, considering our ages and current health. So we'd like to pay for another night."

"Coming." She pulled the book from the chest and dug a little more until she found Wim's solstice plans. There was a by-the-hour list of what needed to go into the oven when, from the pork to the bread and even a mention of shortbread and ginger cake from the Mackeys. She folded it and tucked it inside the book, picked up the glowing stick, and closed the steamer trunk. Perhaps when the solstice was over, she might find time to go through everything up here. There was no telling what other treasures she might find.

Chapter Five

Bev thought better about asking the guests to write their name in the book right away, instead heading into the kitchen to wash her hands and start dinner preparations. The cinnamon roll dough was nearly finished proofing, as was the rosemary bread (though she wanted a second proof on that).

"Bev?" Estera poked her head in. "Oh, goodness. What a smell. That's... What are you making in here?"

"Cinnamon rolls," Bev said, smoothing the cinnamon, sugar, and butter mixture out onto the dough. "Not a typical event here at the Weary Dragon, but considering we're all stuck here another night, I thought it might be a good idea to whip some up."

"You're a saint," she said, standing on the other side of the table.

Bev watched her for a moment, trying to figure out if *she* was the one who'd sent the letter to the Witzels. Estera couldn't have been older than twenty-two, with that youthful sort of air that told of an adult who wasn't quite ready to call themselves such yet.

"So," Bev said, after a moment, "you said you weren't eager to leave. Where are you headed?"

She sighed. "Home. See my folks for the first time since...um..." She glanced at Bev, the flush coming to her cheeks again. "Since a while."

"I see," Bev said. "Is it a long way?"

"Not really. I haven't been given... Er. Haven't found the time to leave." The young woman twisted her hands together, clearly agitated about something.

"Is everything all right?"

"Yes, I just..." Estera looked around. "They told us not to be so open about it when we traveled along the roads. Can't be too sure who's loyal to whom out here in the country, you know?"

Bev tried not to look intrigued as she gathered the edge of the dough and rolled it on itself. "Oh? Who's they?"

"My…um…bosses."

Bev looked up from her careful rolling. The poor girl's face was now the color of a tomato, and her gaze was anywhere but. For someone keen on being cagey about who they were and where they were going, she was a horrible liar.

Or maybe she's faking it to throw you off the scent.

"Goodness," Bev muttered to herself. She'd been too long in the skulking-about business and was starting to mistrust her own instincts.

"What was that?" Estera asked.

"I said, goodness. Well, you're among friends here in Pigsend." She plastered a smile onto her face. "But I understand your business is your own, and I won't pry. I do, however…" She glanced at the guestbook sitting on the counter. "Well, the local librarian asked me to gather the names of the guests who're in town for this little snowstorm we're having. It's something of a rarity in these parts to have so much snow before the solstice." She finished rolling the dough and grabbed her kitchen knife, wiping it with a little butter to help with the cutting. "If you'd be so kind as to at least sign your name on the first blank page, I know he'd appreciate it."

"Didn't you…get my name yesterday?" Estera said with an inquisitive look.

"Yes, but…" Bev sighed. *This* was why she

hadn't bothered with the darn thing in years. "Well, if you feel inclined to fill out the rest of the information, I know Max would appreciate it. But if not…"

If not, you'll be my prime suspect.

"Well, of course," Bernie said, walking over to the guestbook and opening it to the page Bev had marked. "It looks like this hasn't been used in some time."

"Haven't had a freak snowstorm in some time," Bev said, hoping her little lie would hold. "But you know these local archivists. They like to document *everything*."

Collin signed readily, and Abigail signed for her family, as did Wallace. Bev realized too late that this "brilliant" idea wasn't so brilliant—especially if Paul or Byron were the real culprit. But the peer pressure worked, and after everyone had signed, Estera sidled up to at least hastily sign her name and room number on a blank line, her face a deep red.

"Much appreciated," Bev said, closing the book. "If anyone needs me, I'll be in the kitchen getting dinner ready."

She scurried through the door with the book in hand and quickly compared the writing with the letter the Witzels received. Bev wasn't a handwriting expert by any means, but to her eyes, nothing in the book matched the letter.

"Well, that was a lot of effort for nothing," she muttered, snapping the book shut and going to her basket of potatoes.

She sat on her stool and peeled, lost in thought. Of course, there were others who hadn't signed the book—Byron and Paul, and of course, the Mysterious H in room five. But there was a chance even the ones who'd signed had disguised their handwriting, having seen Bev speaking with the butchers.

Or perhaps it wasn't anyone in the inn at all, and it was someone in Pigsend.

Bev's mind was starting to go in circles, and she didn't like it. When it came to the sinkholes, she hadn't been sure of her path, but she'd trusted her instincts. The soldiers who'd inevitably been the culprits had been on her short list from the very beginning. But with the Harvest Festival mishaps, she'd been completely blindsided by Renault or Claude or whatever his actual name was. The judge had been staying in the inn, showing no clear signs that he was the one behind everything until Bev had uncovered the evidence in his room.

Or rather, Biscuit had uncovered the crime.

Bev paused, glancing down at her laelaps, who was passed out in front of the fire. "Hey, Biscuit."

The creature perked up, unfurling his tongue

and smiling.

"Come here for a second," Bev said, pulling out the letter and letting him sniff it. "Do you know who wrote this?"

He sat down and stared up at her, tilting his head in confusion as his mouth closed.

"I mean, was it someone in the inn?" Bev asked.

Blink.

"Well, I suppose it's a good thing you aren't reacting to the note," Bev said, tucking the letter into her back pocket. "Might be nice to get a break from magical nonsense."

He smiled again, wagging his tail as if expecting a treat.

"Useless," Bev said with a half-smile. "Go back to bed."

But he didn't move, his golden eyes traveling to the potato skins piling up next to Bev. She rolled her eyes and pushed three to the floor, which he gobbled up in seconds.

"That's all you get until dinner," Bev said. "Now back to your nap."

He trotted to the fire, curled up, and fell asleep.

Bev was surprised to see Etheldra and Earl come through the door for dinner, having assumed that the heavy snow would keep them away. But Earl, who'd been working to clear the snowy village roads all day, along with a couple of others in town, said he'd worked up an appetite and couldn't say no to Bev's famous rosemary bread.

"Well, if it's you we have to thank for making it easier to get around town, then please, it's on the house tonight," Bev said.

"What about the roads out of town?" Abigail asked. "Are they looking any better?"

"Can't say they are," Etheldra said, eyeing the children with a wary gaze. "And it's started up again."

Abigail and her husband let out a loud groan, which was somewhat adorably mimicked by their two little boys. The baby strapped to her front, however, kept babbling happily.

"How many rooms you have rented, Bev?" Earl asked as he sat with his bowl of food.

"I'm not quite sure about room five," she said, glancing upstairs. She hadn't wanted to knock on the door and check to see if the Mysterious H had decided to stay, but her hunch was that he had.

"Oh, he's in there," Peter, the older of the Wersts' two boys, said. "He came in yelling at Mama for the baby crying."

Bev furrowed her brow. "Next time that happens, you come see me, okay?"

"It's no big deal," Abigail said, waving her hand and looking quite harried. "But I do wish this weather would cooperate so we can get on our way."

"As do we all," Collin said with a sigh. "But in the meantime, I figure I could play a song? Anyone have any recommendations?"

The mood was decidedly *less* festive this evening, but Wallace still called out song after song, and Bev had to admit the music was nice. She ate her meal in silence, watching each of the guests and wondering who could be the one trying to blackmail the Witzels.

Of course, Estera was still top of the list, considering how strange she'd been acting. But would someone so horrible at lying be so brazen as to leave a letter like that?

Bernie, she hadn't had a chance to chat with much, but he seemed to have found a like-minded friend in Estera. Perhaps they'd only come separately, but they were really working together on some devious plan.

To do what?

Bev shook her head. She had to remind herself of the advice she'd given Vellora to look at the big picture.

Collin and Wallace were another pair of fast friends, with poor Paul off to the side reading a book before giving up and going to bed. On the other side of the room, Abigail and Byron seemed too focused on keeping their kids from making a mess. Any one of them could have a motive if she thought about it hard enough.

Don't be ridiculous. It can't be the parents. Bev scoffed.

There was no way they could juggle a gaggle of children *plus* want to shake down the butchers next door.

You thought the same about Claude.

She made a noise and stabbed a potato with her fork.

"You seem distressed, my child," Wallace said, walking up to her with his hands clasped. His breath smelled of ale, and his eyes were a bit more watery than usual. Bev didn't usually charge by the tankard, but she had a feeling if she didn't start curbing the old cleric's drinks, she'd be out of beer before the week was done. "Maybe I can be of service?"

"Just trying to figure something out," Bev said. "And unfortunately, I've lost a bit of my confidence in my own deduction abilities."

"Ah, well—Oh!" Wallace turned, alarmed by the absence of music as he drunkenly toyed with his ring. "Why don't you play another round of *Winter, Winter, Come Hither*?"

"Thanks for the advice," Bev said with a shake of her head.

"I do hope this…young man and his music aren't to be a permanent installation here," Etheldra said, bringing her dirty plate and empty tankard to Bev.

"He's stuck here in town like everyone else," Bev said, taking it. She eyed Etheldra for a moment, briefly reconsidering a Pigsend citizen as the writer of the letter, as preposterous as it sounded.

"What are you staring at?" Etheldra barked.

"Nothing," Bev said. "Get home safely. It's nasty out there."

"Harrumph." She wrapped herself in her cloak and headed for the door as Earl took her place.

"What'd you say to the old bird to get her riled up? Promise to stop making bread?" He chuckled. "Or breathe wrong in her direction?"

"You've been around town for a long time, right, Earl?" Bev said.

He nodded. "All my life. Took over for my dad when he retired."

"And you…" Bev chewed her lip. "I mean, you know the Witzels, right?"

He tilted his head. "You all right there, Bev? Of course I know the Witzels. Why?"

She let out an exasperated breath. "I don't even know, to be honest. I'm trying to figure something out, and I can't seem to get my head on straight. Don't know the questions to ask." She paused. "I guess the real question is: the people of Pigsend, we stick together, right? I'm not imagining that?"

"Is this about the sinkholes?" Earl asked. "Everyone's moved on from that, especially after you saved the Harvest Festival."

Bev finally decided to let it go. "Never mind, Earl. The snow's getting to my head, I'm sure. Have a safe walk home, and hopefully the weather will clear."

He tipped his cap to her, though there was still a bit of wariness in his gaze. "Get some rest, Bev. You look like you need it."

Unfortunately, two guests decided to make a late night of it, with Wallace calling out more songs for Collin to play until Abigail made an appearance at the top of the stairs and gave them *one very clear look* to quiet down or else.

"Suppose that's it, eh?" Wallace said, slowly getting up and rubbing his stomach. "Well, Collin, in the morning!"

"In the morning," the bard said with a small smile. He seemed to be waiting for something from the old cleric, but the other man simply walked up the stairs, humming the solstice melodies to himself all the way to his room.

"I bet your fingers are tired," Bev said, absentmindedly wiping the counters. "But before you head to bed, I hate to ask, but I don't think I've gotten your silver from you for tonight."

"Well, um…" Collin rubbed the back of his neck. "You see…"

Bev quirked a brow.

"I don't exactly *have* the money to stay another night right now. I'm sure I could, in a couple of days, but…" He coughed. "I really wasn't planning on staying. But it seems I *have* to. So um…" He grinned sheepishly. "I was hoping we might barter? Music for a bed?"

"That's a barter you needed to ask about when there was daylight," Bev said, a little tersely. Every so often, she'd get a patron like this, who'd try to sneak by with a free night. Though she could give Collin a bit of leeway due to the weather, it still struck her as rude.

"I'd be happy to pay you on my way back," Collin said. "Once I've gotten my payment from Kaiser Tuckey, of course. And there would be interest, too."

"Listen, how about this: if you'll help me clean up tonight, I'll let you off the hook. But I want that kitchen *spotless* when I come back there, understood? I'm not one to throw a man out in the cold, but I'm also not to be messed with."

He nodded, reaching for his cuffs and rolling them up. "Spotless, it'll be!"

"But before that," Bev said, "I want you to walk up to room five and tell him he needs to pay for his room."

Collin blanched. "I don't want to talk to *him*."

"Neither do I, so hurry on up there." Bev chuckled. "And then come on down and get to work on the dishes."

The bard climbed the stairs, and Bev listened as he knocked on the door, the disgruntled voice that followed, then the door slam—waking the baby next door. A few moments later, Collin walked back down the stairs, wincing with every step and holding a gold coin.

"He gave me this," he said. "Do you think it could cover—"

"Nope." Bev thumbed toward the kitchen. "Get to work."

CHAPTER SIX

Bev was too tired to stay up and ensure Collin did a good job in the kitchen, so she and Biscuit called it a night, hoping that in the morning, the snow would miraculously disappear, and her collection of guests would be able to depart. But when she awoke, there seemed to be even *more* snow on the ground than the night before, hiding the footprints Bev had made going to and from the stables.

"Perfect," she muttered, going to the wash basin and getting started with her day.

The kitchen was passable, and at least a good chunk of things were ready to go. Bev trudged out to check on the animals out back, finding the snow past her knees now. Biscuit took one look at the snow and promptly returned to the fire.

The old mule seemed all right inside the stable, but Bev still put another blanket over her back to keep her warm. Bev doubted Sin would mind a few extra days of rest anyway. The horse seemed to be of the same mindset, so Bev left lots of hay and oats, along with a couple of carrots and fresh water, before heading back to the kitchen.

Bev set to her morning chores in the kitchen, finishing up the details Collin had missed, and saying a small prayer of thanks she'd thought to replenish all her stores well in advance of the solstice. She had plenty of vegetables and flour, and the walk to the butcher shop was short.

Though thinking of the butchers reminded Bev of the mysterious letter they'd received. Bev knew they hadn't done as instructed and left gold on their back step, so it remained to be seen if the blackmailer would continue their threats or not. Hopefully, they'd see the error of their ways and stop.

Estera was the first one down the stairs, rubbing her eyes with her bag slung around her neck. She caught Bev's gaze and offered a half-smile.

"How's it looking out there?" she asked, walking into the kitchen.

"Not great," Bev said. "More snow fell. I think we're in for another day of the same."

"And five days until the solstice," she said with a shake of her head. "I don't think I'll be making it at this rate."

"Going home, right?" Bev asked, hoping to get more out of her.

She nodded. "You know, my mom used to bake bread like this every day, too. She'd have—" Estera walked over to the counter where the jar of starter and barm sat. "That's it. The starter. Though yours smells different."

"I think they all take on their own unique tastes," Bev said, working the dough. "But you seem to be making yourself at home all right here. Making friends."

"Somewhat." She cracked a nervous smile. "Just being polite. We're all stuck here."

"You and Bernie seem to be hitting it off."

"I wouldn't say that," she said. "He's nice enough. But there weren't too many folks to talk with last night, what with that family and the loud bard and the clergyman's husband." She shuddered. "He seems to have a bad attitude."

"Paul?" Bev chuckled. "I try not to disparage my guests. But he's a dreamboat compared to the man in room five."

"Bernie told me about him, but I haven't met

him myself," she said. "I think I'd prefer…"

A loud stomping echoed down the stairs, and Bev put her finger to her lips as the Mysterious H appeared, still wrapped head-to-toe in his coverings. He said nothing to the two of them, walking straight out the door.

"Well, I suppose that's the last we'll see of him," Estera said. "Seems keen on leaving."

"I'm not sure how successful he'll be," Bev said. "All the work Earl did yesterday shoveling the roads seems to be for naught."

"I hope he does leave. He's certainly not the brightest ray of sunshine."

"Agreed." He was suspicious, of course, and if it weren't for his insistence on leaving, Bev would've thought he was the one blackmailing the Witzels. She turned to Estera, trying for a neutral expression. "But I suppose one could say the same of you. You're pretty reticent to say where you're traveling from."

She exhaled, her shoulders slouching. "Well, that's…a safety issue, really."

"Is it?" Bev frowned. "Who could possibly want to harm you? You're such a dear."

"It's not me, per se, but…" She lowered her voice to a whisper. "I'm a member of the queen's service."

Bev nearly missed the knead on the dough. *That*

was a bit of juicy information. "You are? But you're so young."

"Well, I'm not a bigwig or anything. Just a foot soldier." She cleared her throat. "My commander said it's dangerous for queenside soldiers to travel alone, especially ones who, uh..." Her cheeks went pink again. "Who can't really defend themselves all that well."

"I'm sure you do fine," Bev said. Oh, but if Vellora knew... "But the queen's people won. Why would they be worried about your safety?"

"A lot of kingside soldiers settled down out here in the country," she said. "In fact, that's what Bernie and I were discussing last night."

"Is he queenside?"

"He said he didn't fight," she said. "But he'd been here a bit longer than me, so I asked him if there were any kingside soldiers around, and he said the roads were full of 'em. No telling who might be hiding their true identity. Just waiting to find an innocent queenside soldier, and—" She made a squelching sound.

"Well, I doubt you'll have to worry about that here," Bev said. "But I understand why you don't want folks to know your business. Still...you couldn't be old enough to have fought in the war."

"No, I joined two years ago," she said. "And only because there weren't any jobs in my small village, and I wanted to travel. But I didn't realize I'd be stuck with them for every holiday. This is the first time I've been granted leave—and it's only because I promised them I'd be a short ride away."

Bev started. "There aren't any soldiers around here, are there? Other than you, I mean?"

Again, she hesitated, which told Bev everything she needed to know.

"I mean, my group isn't *big* per se," Estera said, after a too-long pause. "But they are kind of close. At least they were. Probably moved on by now. You know."

She laughed nervously as Bev watched her carefully. Her story was believable. She was very young, and she seemed to wear her emotions on her face. But it could also be a carefully constructed lie, like Claude's had been.

Their conversation came to an abrupt halt when the front door swung open and the Mysterious H returned, brushing snow off his shoulders angrily. His dark eyes met Bev's through the open kitchen door, and he approached with all the ferocity of a summer storm.

"Is it another gold coin to stay the night?"

That little weasel. Collin must've upped the price. "I'm offering a silver, since we're all stuck here anyway," Bev said.

He reached into his coin purse and placed a gold

down on the kitchen table. "If anyone asks for me, I'm not here. Do you understand?"

"I'm not sure I know enough about you to say anything to anyone," Bev said. "But I'll be sure to keep your appearance under wraps. As long as you keep your temper with the children in room six. Those poor parents have enough to deal with, keeping their kids from going crazy. I don't want to hear anything else about you haranguing them for their baby crying."

He eyed her, almost daring her to keep talking. But Bev held his gaze. After all, he could leave. Wouldn't make her lose any sleep at night.

"Fine." He all but spat the word. "I'll be returning to my room for the evening."

"Would you like me to bring you a plate of food? It's been a few days since you've eaten."

"I've managed." He turned on his heel and walked upstairs without another word.

"Brr," Estera said with an overdramatic shake. "Maybe *he's* the reason the snow keeps falling, what with his chilly disposition."

Bev chuckled, but it wasn't as far-fetched as it sounded. "I'll say a prayer we get some warmer weather so you can all get on your way. In the meantime, hopefully, the baker will be bringing by some goodies for breakfast soon. That might take some of the edge off having to stay another day."

Even Allen's sugar-coated, jam-filled pastries were no match for the angst that came with finding out the snow had yet again made travel impossible. Bev paid special attention to those who weren't all that upset about the news, though her focus never really left Estera.

A queen's soldier could definitely be the one blackmailing the Witzels. Estera's clothes were a bit on the threadbare side, but perhaps because she didn't need many civilian clothes and *not* because she was in desperate need of money. But she was clearly uncomfortable talking about her regiment—and there was a good chance they were still close, with as cagey as she was acting.

For the moment, though, the young woman seemed relaxed in the front room, entertaining the two Werst boys with a clapping game while their father looked on, enjoying his small break.

Bev finally tore her gaze away from them, noting the time and remembering she still had baking to do. She and Biscuit returned to the warm kitchen, and she'd just retrieved her dough from its proofing spot when the back door opened and Ida stepped in, dusting snow from her shoulders.

"Hey." Ida shook off her cloak. "I figured I'd come to you to get your order this morning. And maybe…get an update on everything." She glanced behind Bev at the closed door. "How goes it?"

"Oh fine," Bev said, deciding against telling Ida her discovery of Estera until she knew more. "Nothing to report."

But Ida stepped in front of her, narrowing her gaze. "You're hiding something."

"I am not." Bev put the bread into its proofing baskets without meeting her gaze. "What makes you say that?"

"Because I know you." Ida crossed the kitchen. "What did you find? Did everyone sign the guestbook?"

"They did," Bev said. "Results inconclusive."

"What does that mean?"

"It means that nobody's handwriting matched," Bev said. "And I don't have any news for you."

"Don't you?" Ida put her hands on her hips.

Bev let out a breath. "*Fine*, I might have a few things. But you absolutely *cannot* tell your wife. I'm not quite sure what it means, and I don't want her coming over here and flying off the handle. Got it?"

Ida stepped closer, grinning. "What is it?"

"Well, one of the guests is apparently a queen's soldier," Bev said, deciding to share only the information she knew was true. "She's young, though. Barely twenty. Just signed up two years ago. I sincerely doubt she's the one who sent you the letter."

"Nobody had any doubts about Claude, either," Ida muttered.

Bev started. "You keep feeling that way, too? I swear, it's like I've lost my ability to trust people. I'm even side-eyeing the mother of three and wondering what secrets *she* has up her sleeve. But she's barely got time to keep her own head on straight." She sighed. "I hate this feeling. It's not nice."

"I know." Ida leaned on the counter. "I don't like it either. I guess I'm starting to understand my wife's paranoia a bit more. But also..." She leaned in. "A queen's soldier would have a pretty good motive. All she'd have to do was return to her commander and tell him I'm here."

"But she'd have to be able to return to him," Bev said, cleaning her hands in the basin. She crossed the room to retrieve the guestbook and letter and placed both in front of Ida. "Look, see? The letter appears more like chicken scratch. Estera's handwriting is much loopier. I don't see how we can definitively pin this on her."

"Unless she wrote it with her left hand to throw us off," Ida said.

There was some small comfort that Ida had the same doubts as Bev. "Give me time to talk with her. I think she's starting to trust me now. I might be able to get more out of her since we're all stuck here another day."

"Keep me posted," Ida said, walking to the door. She was almost through it when she stopped and turned around. "Oh. What do you want to buy from us today? I've got more beef or maybe I can rustle up some sausages."

"Let's do beef," Bev said. "And remember: not a word to your wife about this until I know more."

Ida saluted like a soldier and walked through the back door.

Bev plotted all morning how she might get the young soldier alone to talk with her more, but the soldier seemed to have ingratiated herself with the Wersts, especially the two little boys. Bev listened to them play clapping games and singing games all morning until finally walking through the kitchen to play in the snowy back yard. Bev watched them romp and play, unable to find any scrap of deception in Estera's joyful face. She actually appeared *happier* than she had in the past few days. So perhaps not the blackmailer, but—

Bev blinked as a large figure came barreling into the yard, right up to Estera and picking the young soldier up by the front of her shirt.

"Oh, *goodness!*" Bev muttered, throwing down her towel and grabbing her cloak as she ran outside. "Vellora, put her down this instant!"

"Not until I get my answer, Bev," Vellora bellowed, all but shaking the poor girl. "*Did you write the letter?*"

"I don't know what you're talking about!" Estera cried, tears streaming down her bright red face. "Bev! Help! Who is this?"

Bev turned to the two little boys, who were cowering behind their snowman. "Go back inside, boys. Find your mom."

They didn't need to be told twice, running as fast as their little legs would carry them.

"Vellora, *put her down*," Bev said, grabbing Vellora's thick arm and pulling on it. But the butcher was much stronger, and kept her grip. "She's innocent—"

"Nobody in the queen's service is innocent," Vellora said, shaking the girl again. "*Tell me why you wrote that letter!*"

"*Vellora Witzel.*" Ida cried, dashing into the yard. And, of course, when Ida pulled, Vellora's grip relented, dumping Estera unceremoniously to the ground. "I *told* you to cool it!"

"Not until I know for sure if this little *weasel* is the one threatening us!" Vellora snarled, leaning down toward the trembling girl.

"I think you should take Vellora home," Bev barked at Ida with a dirty glare. "You promised—"

"It slipped," Ida said with a shrug.

"W-what are you… What's going on?" Estera, her clothes a mess, was shaking as she scrambled to her feet. "Who in the world are these people? What do they want with me?" She turned to Bev. "Did you… Did you tell them who I was?"

"I mentioned it, but only because—"

"I *told* you it was dangerous for people to know who I am!" Estera said, her eyes filled with tears as she backed up, gripping her clothes. Then, without another word, she dashed toward the inn, leaving a heaving Bev with the two butchers.

Bev whirled toward Ida, furious. "Now see what you've done? Vellora's scared the poor girl half to death."

"She deserves it," Vellora said.

"She clearly didn't write the letter." Bev rolled her eyes.

"A likely—"

"Darling," Ida said gently, putting her hand on Vellora's arm, "I don't think you can fake that kind of fear. You scared the daylights out of her."

"Well, good!" Vellora huffed.

"Go back home," Ida said. "I'll find her and apologize—"

"You'll do no such thing," Bev said, holding up her hands. "You've done enough for today. Both of you. I'll be by later to pick up my order, but the two of you had better steer clear of the inn."

"What in the world is going on out here?" Byron came running outside. "The boys said—" He took one look at Vellora and swallowed hard. They were perhaps the same height, but Vellora weighed about three times as much as he did. "Um. The boys said there was trouble."

"No trouble at all," Bev said, giving the sheepish butchers another glare. "Now if you'll excuse me, I'm going to check on Estera and make her a nice cup of tea."

~

When Bev knocked on Estera's door, there was no answer—but it did swing open. Bev poked her head inside and found it completely empty. The soldier was gone.

"Ah, she wanted me to tell you she was leaving," Bernie said, appearing in his doorway. "Seemed spooked about something, poor girl. Did I hear yelling outside?"

"A misunderstanding," Bev said, a little sadly. "Well, I know she wanted to get on her way. Maybe she'll be able to make it to the next town before nightfall."

CHAPTER SEVEN

Bev was agitated all day about the butchers betraying her trust and potentially sending a young, innocent soldier out into the elements. Ida meekly brought Bev the beef she'd ordered—and didn't take the payment—but Bev said nothing to her, even as she apologized again for her wife.

"I didn't think she'd go... I didn't believe she'd fly off the handle like that," Ida said. "If you want, I can go looking for that soldier—"

Bev shook her head. "Let's just pray she gets somewhere safely."

Ida nodded, leaving Bev alone with her guilty thoughts. Because at the end of the day, it was *Bev* who'd told Ida, knowing full well that the Witzels shared everything, as married couples did. So there really was no one to blame but herself.

The weather held until night fell, and for that, Bev was grateful. She did her best to forget about the soldier, hoping the poor girl was at least somewhere safe and warm. There was nothing she could do about it now, and since the Witzels hadn't gotten another threatening letter, it was best to put the whole business behind them.

Dinner was another night filled with Collin singing Wallace's suggestions. Bev briefly saw Etheldra and Earl's faces in the doorway, but they heard the music and promptly turned around to go back home. Bev chuckled, but also made sure to quell the singing and debauchery well before eight so the Wersts could get their exhausted children to bed—and so Collin, who yet again had no coin to pay for his room, could start on cleaning the kitchen for her.

While he worked, Bev sat in the empty front hall, listening to the fire crackle as she ensured everyone had paid their silver for the night—or in the case of the Mysterious H, a gold. It felt like it had been a week since the early morning when he'd last been seen. Amazing the things that happened when a group of people were all but trapped in a small inn.

Finally, when her own eyelids started to droop, she popped into the kitchen where Collin was scrubbing her large iron pot.

"I'm headed to bed," Bev said.

"It looks to be snowing again," Collin said, leaning his head to look at the window. "Wild weather, huh?"

She stifled a groan. "Indeed. Good night, Collin."

There was, indeed, *more* snow on the ground when she awoke the next day, and not even chipper Bev could hold in the groan. Besides her tenants needing to stay another day, she also still had to check on Herman's goats. It had been three days since she'd last refreshed their food and water, and they were probably running low.

"Well, Bev ol' girl, gotta earn your gold somehow."

She wrapped herself up in sweaters and put on thick wool socks under her boots. The road was long, and the sun was all the way up by the time she reached the house. She didn't have time to check the house itself, but from a distance, it looked fine. The goats seemed to be working through their hay and water slowly, but Bev replenished it anyway. No telling when she'd be able to get back out here—she wasn't eager to trudge through knee-high snow again.

When she returned to the inn, it was nearly ten in the morning, and the guests had come to the same conclusion about the condition of the roads. Even Bernie, who seemed unruffled by anything, was a bit on the grumpy side when Bev gave her report on how it was to get down the road.

"This is why I prefer the southern country," he said, with a roll of his eyes.

"I wish I could fix it," Bev said apologetically. "Does anyone think they might want to make a break for it?"

"I don't see Estera among our number anymore," Paul said. "Where did she go?"

"I believe the pull of her mother's home was too strong," Bev said, hoping her face didn't betray her lie. "Obviously, I'm not going to keep anyone here against their will. But it is a mess out there."

"Looks like that Earl fellow is hard at work on the streets again," Paul said, standing near the window. "Perhaps it might be all right to take a turn around the village. Is there any kind of entertainment in town?"

"The bard isn't enough for you?" Byron muttered, earning a chuckle from his wife.

"Actually!" Bev brightened. "We have something of a small library in town. Might not be much for the boys, but it could be somewhere to go that's not, well, here."

Abigail smiled. "I think we'd love that."

"A library, you said?" Bernie asked, with Paul on his heels. "In a town this size?"

"Don't get too excited," Bev said. "It's mostly almanacs and recorded history. But you might be able to find something there that'll distract you from these four walls."

The traveling entourage included all five Wersts, Bernie, Paul, and Bev trailing the rest. Bev's so-called *loyal* dog seemed eager to stay indoors with all the snow, so she left him snoozing in front of the fire. Wallace and Collin hadn't been seen yet, but Bev left a few of Allen's pastries in the basket for whenever they did rouse.

The roads were a slushy, sloppy mess—a combination of Earl's attempts to shovel them plus the new snow and old mixing. Byron carried the younger of his sons on his shoulder while Bernie happily chatted with the older, and Abigail kept her baby girl strapped to her front. Paul huffed and puffed, but Bev stayed a few steps behind him to make sure he didn't lose his footing.

"Would be nice if someone carried me," he said with a half-smile.

Bev nodded as they passed the Witzel butcher shop. The two women were inside hard at work, and Bev purposefully didn't look inside. She was still angry with them for scaring off Estera, but eventually she'd have to swallow her anger and buy some more meat or the inn would go hungry.

"It really is a quaint little village," Paul said as they continued the slow parade down the street. "I'm sure it's lovely in the spring when there isn't so much snow on the ground."

"Can't remember a time when it was this bad, even in the colder months," Bev said with a small shudder. "But yes, it's a lovely place to live. The people, too."

"Even those butchers?" Paul gave her a look. "I saw what happened yesterday. Looked to be some nasty business."

Bev sighed. "I apologize that you had to see that. And if Estera were still around, I'd apologize to her, too. There's… Well, the butchers are a bit stressed with their upcoming holiday party, and I think it got to their heads."

"Mm."

The library finally appeared in the distance, and the group put on a bit of speed. Closer to the town square, the roads had been shoveled better and walking was much easier. Bev followed the group into the building, waving to the old librarian, Max Sterling.

"Bev! You brought a gaggle today," he said with a bright smile. "Are these all your guests from the

93

inn?"

"They are," she said with a nod. "Looking for something to pass the time."

"Well, we don't have much, but I'm sure I can find a few books that might tickle your fancy." He slid off his stool and walked around the counter. "Come, come."

Bev milled in the front of the library as her guests explored the stacks with Max. She turned to the front windows, watching the snow-covered town square, still void of that dragon statue, and winced, thinking again about her disastrous tea with Ramone and all the little would-be fountain designs on the floor. Perhaps the artist was less annoyed with Bev and more annoyed with themselves for not being able to break through whatever creative rut they were in.

A couple of folks were out and about, but not many. Bev didn't see a fire coming from the town hall, so perhaps Mayor Hendry and Sheriff Rustin weren't in the office. Max lived above the library, so it wasn't much trouble for him to stay open, like Bev. Not that there was usually much activity this time of year around town, but the snow was certainly putting a damper on the usual pre-solstice festivities.

Speaking of… She was still on the hook for the Witzels' party. Despite being annoyed with them, she wouldn't dream of canceling such an important event.

Max came walking back to the front with a smile on his face. "Bev, is there anything I can get for you?"

"Not unless you have a way to clear all this snow," she replied. "Have you seen many folks lately?"

"You know, it's quiet most days around here. I've spent the past few weeks getting the harvest totals from the farmers and adding them to this year's almanac." He showed her the large book he'd been scribbling in when they arrived. "I was working on Alice Estrich's totals for the year just now."

Bev nodded. "Every year, you do this? Is it mandatory?"

And by that, she meant did the queen make him do it? Max seemed to understand and chuckled. "No, this isn't necessarily required by Her Majesty, though with all the ways she's getting her fingers into things, I'm sure it's only a matter of time. But this is how I learned from the previous historian, and how she learned from her predecessor, and so on."

"I can't imagine this sort of thing is useful," Bev said, turning the page slowly. This section seemed to be accounting for births, deaths, weddings, and new folks in the town and immediate surrounding areas. This year, one birth and no deaths, with one wedding and three new townsfolk. "Well, this probably is, but how many pounds the farmers grew?"

"You'd be surprised," Max said. "Some of them like to check on their historical records from year to year. Find out if their current crop is low or if it's just the yield from whatever field they opted for. Having all the records in one place is useful to them."

Bev nodded; she wasn't a farmer, so she hadn't thought of it that way. She flipped back another page and saw a list of notable events for the year. Included were a few paragraphs on the sinkhole debacle and this year's almost-canceled Harvest Festival.

"I've still got to update that page to include all this snow," Max said with a shake of his head. "That's certainly something to remember."

"I'd rather forget it already," Bev said with a laugh. "You do all this recording by yourself every year?"

"My nephew comes from Middleburg for the solstice to help me get it all done, but I'm sure he's been deterred by the snow like everyone else."

Bev smiled. "I didn't realize you had a nephew."

"Oh, he usually comes for a day or two then

leaves. It's not exciting work, this archival stuff. Once I'm done with the almanac, I've got to update the town family trees. Luckily, it's not much this year."

"Does everyone get a family tree?" Bev asked. She certainly would have a short one, if he'd made one for her.

"It's rare I make a new one, since most folks end up marrying into a family," Max said. "And if they're like you, they're recorded in the town annals." He coughed, a little nervously. "A-alone, I meant."

"I'm happy to be alone, Max," she said. "Though I suppose one could make a tree and include Biscuit on it…but that seems a bit much."

He chuckled. "Indeed. Take Vellora Witzel, for example. She married into the Witzel family, so I merely added her to their tree." He paused. "Actually, Ida was in here recently, looking up her family history, and she complimented me on the detail and accuracy of her tree." He beamed. "I'm glad we have these resources available to her and others."

"Others?" Bev furrowed her brow. "Who else has been in here looking up their family information?"

"Well, Grant Klose's cousin, Jasper, was in here a few times before all the snow fell. Haven't seen him since, though."

"What was he looking for?" Bev asked, trying to sound nonchalant.

"Same as Ida. The Kloses are distant relatives of the Witzels," he said. "Ida's great-grandfather and their great-grandfather were brothers, if memory serves."

Grant was nice enough—a farmer who lived on the west side of town and a regular at the twice-weekly farmers' market. Ida had mentioned she was distantly related to a couple of folks in town but hadn't ever mentioned Grant specifically. Perhaps she didn't know.

"What was he looking for?"

"I'm not exactly sure, to be honest." He tilted his head. "Why?"

"Just curious," Bev said. After all, there hadn't been another letter to the Witzels since the first one.

Perhaps if Jasper Klose had written it, he was too busy being stuck inside his cousin's house. But Bev still tucked that bit of information in her back pocket. Just in case something else came up.

Her gaggle of guests were ready to leave, laden with what remained of Max's fiction collection. Paul, especially, had a large stack and for the first time, the cleric's husband looked happy. Max even had a few children's books for the boys, who were eager to get back and have their mother read to them.

"I'll make sure these all get returned to you," Bev said.

"Like that book you borrowed three months ago?" Max said with a wink. "It's fine. Better I don't have it, I'm sure."

Bev smiled. It was a book about magical creatures and had come in handy several times over the past few months. She wasn't ready to give it back quite yet. She thanked Max for his generosity and wished him a happy solstice, if she didn't see him again before the blessed event.

"Oh, I hear the Witzels are throwing a party at the inn?" he said. "Ida invited me, so I'm sure I'll see you then."

"Great," Bev said. "Have a good one, Max."

Holding their treasures tight, the group made their way toward the Weary Dragon, with Bev once again taking the rear. The sun was threatening to peek between the dull gray clouds, but the slushy mess was still difficult to walk through—even more so with all the books the guests carried. But they wouldn't be deterred, and Bev had a feeling that a bit of time outside the inn had turned more than a few sour moods—it had certainly made her less annoyed.

The Witzel butcher shop was coming up, and Bev realized she'd have to talk to the butchers sooner rather than later. With a sigh, she shook her shoulders and smiled at Paul and Bernie, who were walking side by side with her.

"If you two will make sure the group makes it back to the inn, I've got to stop in here to put in my meat order for the evening."

"Oh, could we do lamb tonight?" Bernie asked.

"It depends on what they have," Bev replied with a shrug. "They may still be working through the beef, but we might be able to get some sausage. I'll see what I can do."

"Excellent." He smiled. "Not that I don't love a good beef stew, but..."

"But three nights in a row is a bit excessive," Bev said with a knowing nod as she peeled away. "Be back soon!"

She continued walking down the now unshoveled path until she reached the Witzels' front door and pushed it open with some difficulty. The butchers weren't in the front room, but she hadn't expected them to be.

"Vellora? Ida?" Bev called, walking up to the counter. "Are you guys here?"

Footsteps echoed from above, and Ida took the back stairs slowly. Her face was a mask of uncertainty, and she kept her gaze on the ground.

"Ida, about yesterday—"

"Clearly, it wasn't the soldier because..." She lifted a folded letter. "We got another letter."

My patience is wearing thin and the price has gone up.

Seventy-five gold coins on your back step tonight, or I go to the soldiers with what I know of your crimes.

CHAPTER EIGHT

"What soldiers do you think they're talking about?" Vellora asked. "There aren't any in town."

"Not anymore," Bev said, swallowing the snarky *Thanks to you*. "But Estera told me her regiment was close. Clearly, the blackmailer thinks they still are. Doubtful they're traveling in this mess."

"But the snow will melt eventually," Vellora said, pacing in front of the fire. "And at that point, if we don't do what this blackmailer says, they can ride up to the soldiers, tell them...whatever it is they're going to tell them, and if we don't get the heck out of here—"

"We're not going anywhere," Ida said with a

stern look. "This is our *home*. And we aren't going to be scared off because…" She cleared her throat. "I don't even know what *crimes* they're referring to. We've done nothing wrong."

"Exactly," Bev said. "Which is why I think you need to take this to Rustin."

The butchers shared a look, and Vellora spoke first, "Absolutely not. Leave him out of this."

"He won't do anything even if we tell him," Ida said with a firm nod.

"It might scare away whoever is sending these, though," Bev said. "If, as you say, you've nothing to hide, what a show of confidence that you involve the local sheriff. At least it would get the blackmailers to back off."

"We still have no idea who it might be?" Vellora asked.

"Clearly, it's not Estera," Bev said. "She was long gone by the time you got this. It could be someone from the inn, but it's hard for me to tell who's coming and going. Or it…" She sighed. "It could be Grant Klose's cousin."

"Who?" Ida blinked. "Grant… Grant, like farmer Grant? His cousin? What in the…"

Bev briefly explained what Max had said about Jasper Klose looking through the family trees, and Vellora smacked her hand on the counter.

"That little *weasel!*" She marched toward her

cloak.

"Vellora," Bev said, her tone a warning, "we're not doing that again."

"Doing what?"

"Accusing people without proof," Bev said. "Or do you not want my help?"

Vellora hesitated for a moment before dropping her arm. "Fine."

"Ida, what do you know about the Kloses?" Bev asked. "Max said that Grant's great-grandfather and yours were brothers?"

She nodded. "It's something of a family scandal, actually. My great-great-grandparents Magdalena and Lombard settled in Pigsend and started this butcher shop." She looked around with a smile. "Built these walls themselves, along with their two young sons, Keven and my great-grandfather Adel. They were close in age, but my great-grandfather was the younger of the two. The butcher shop was successful, of course, but when Magdalena and Lombard died, there was a bit of a…um… controversy. Now, I only know our side of the story, so please take this with a grain of salt, but…"

"Go on," Bev said.

"Apparently, Keven was something of a lazy clod. He would skip town to chase skirts and drink away his salary. So when their parents died, they left the butcher shop to Adel. Of course, Keven contested the will, brought in some kind of fancy lawyer. But the will was very clear, or at least he was unsuccessful in getting it overturned." She shrugged. "So Keven packed up and left for Middleburg to make his fortunes there. He married a woman, had a daughter—Grant Klose's grandmother, and...well, that's that." She shrugged. "I know the Kloses have their own butcher shops in Middleburg, but they've always been salty about this place."

"Did any of them have magic?" Bev asked.

"Not to my knowledge," Ida said. "Nobody in our family said anything about it to me if they did."

"It could be possible the Kloses found out about your magic and want to use that as leverage," Vellora said.

Bev shook her head, gesturing to the letter. "They haven't once asked for the shop itself. They want money. It doesn't quite fit, you know?" She tapped her finger on the counter. "But I still think it's worthwhile to take a walk out to Grant's house and talk with them. He and I get along pretty well. Might be able to glean something from him."

"And if not, we can sneak—" Ida began with a devilish grin, but both Bev and Vellora held up their hands to quiet her.

"We are *not* breaking into anyone's house," Bev said.

"Especially since Grant is probably going to be

in said house with his cousin," Vellora said. "I don't even know where they live. Is it far?"

"It's farther with all the snow, but I can manage," Bev said. "First, though, I want to take this letter to Sheriff Rustin. Now, I won't tell him who received it," she began as Ida opened her mouth to argue, "but I think it's important that we at least let him know. I'll see if he's got any ideas. Then, once we've checked that box, I can..." She grimaced. "Head out to Grant's house and talk with his cousin. But only if the snow melts a little." She shook her head. "Can't believe someone would willingly be out in all this to harass people."

"Unless they're sure they've got a good reason to harass people." Vellora crossed her arms over her chest. "Fine. Loop in Rustin. And talk with the Kloses. But in the meantime, who's going to be keeping an eye on the possible suspects at the inn?"

"Well, Ida..." Bev turned to the other butcher. "You still need to decorate the tree, don't you?"

"Oh, Bev, that's a brilliant idea," Ida said with a smile.

"I'll be back as soon as I can." She paused. "I know you've got a lot to worry about right now, but I also need meat for dinner."

Vellora snorted. "Don't worry, slicing up some meat is the thing to take my mind off all this."

"At least it's already dead," Ida replied with a

dark chuckle. "Bev... Thank you for looking into this for us. And not...um..." She rubbed the back of her neck. "Well, thanks."

"Don't mention it." Bev gave them both a firm smile. "We'll figure this out. You two aren't going anywhere if I have anything to do with it."

~

With the second letter tucked under her arm, Bev returned to the Weary Dragon. The front room was filled, but quiet as everyone with a book was nose-deep in it. Bev didn't see Collin or Wallace yet, which she noted in her mental list of suspects. The bread was rising nicely, and if she left now, she could make it to Rustin's house before she needed to tend to it again.

"Biscuit, you want to go for a walk?" she asked the laelaps sleeping by the fire.

He lifted his head for a moment before going back to sleep.

She hadn't yet changed out of her traveling clothes, so she grabbed the first letter and tucked it into her cloak with the second then headed straight out the door.

Rustin lived on the west side of town, a few streets up from Bev. It was a short walk on a normal day, but as Bev had discovered, the snow made quick trips anything but. She reached his door and knocked loudly. When there was no answer, she knocked again, harder. A third time finally earned her some noise from the other side of the wall. The door opened, and Rustin, sporting an uncharacteristic stubble and scowl, appeared wearing what appeared to be his dressing robe.

"B-Bev? What in the world are you doing here?" He rubbed the back of his head. "I…uh…with the snow, it's…uh…"

"I'm not here to ask why you aren't at your desk," Bev said with a smile. "Look, I hate to bug you with this so close to the solstice, but a… Well, someone in town is receiving threatening letters." She handed them over. "The recipient wanted to remain anonymous, but I thought it was important that you know."

He read through the letters with the same sort of skepticism she'd had. "Er… What does this…uh, blackmailer think the crimes are?"

"We aren't quite sure," Bev said. "The recipient doesn't seem to know what they're talking about either."

"And they've done nothing wrong?"

"Not to our knowledge, no."

"Then I say ignore it," Rustin said, handing Bev the letters back. "There's too much dang snow on the ground to do anything about it anyway."

Bev hesitated. "I think they're worried because there's a regiment of queen's soldiers just north of here."

"You said they'd done nothing wrong."

"Yes, but…" Bev was trying to be delicate. "You know, sometimes a person can have *done* nothing wrong and still get in trouble. Especially where the queen is concerned."

He lifted a shoulder, as if that didn't really faze him. "I still say that if there's nothing to worry about, there's nothing to worry about. Probably someone who got bored sitting around waiting for the snow to melt. If they get another one when the snow's gone, *then* we can worry." He smiled. "I suppose I'll see you at the Witzel solstice party in a couple of days!"

Bev offered a half-smile. "Yes, indeed. Thanks for the advice, Rustin."

~

When she returned to the inn, Ida was there decorating the solstice tree. Already, the entire front room looked more festive, with red-berried holly and sprigs of mistletoe hung around the room. Wallace had finally made his appearance and was helping Ida hang multicolored baubles from the branches, while the little boys fetched them from the boxes.

"Was this your idea?" Abigail asked, walking up to Bev. "The boys were devastated that we weren't going to be able to do a solstice tree since we were traveling."

"Yes and no," Bev said. "Ida's throwing her annual solstice party here in a couple of days, so she wanted to decorate in advance of that. But I'm glad your boys are getting their holiday cheer."

"You've been so patient with us," Abigail said, taking Bev's hand. "I want you to know it's appreciated. Greatly. How is it looking out there?"

Bev hated to tell her the truth. "It's still pretty rough. I walked to the local sheriff's house just now, and it wasn't very easy. You're the ones with the horse in the barn, right?"

She nodded. "Byron went out to check on the wagon yesterday. It's good and stuck until some of this snow melts." She sighed, looking down at the sleeping infant strapped to her front. "I think the boys would be fine, but I worry about the baby." She let out a small chuckle. "Serves me right for tempting fate. First major snowfall in this region before the solstice in years."

"Sometimes, that's how it goes," Bev said. "But you're welcome here, and the boys are fine. I'm glad we have space for the five of you."

Pascal, the younger of the two, let out a gasp as he dropped one of the baubles and it smashed into a hundred pieces.

"Oh, goodness," Abigail muttered, rushing toward him to get him away from the shards. "Let me pay for that, please."

"I have a hundred of them," Ida replied, waving her hand. "I wouldn't have let them help if they were truly sentimental. I've been around kids before."

Abigail gave her a relieved smile as Bev left in search of her broom and dustpan. When she returned, Abigail insisted on cleaning up the mess, while little Pascal held the pan. When it was all clean, the child walked up to Ida and tilted his head back.

"Sowwy."

"It's totally fine, sweetheart," she said, patting him on the head. "Now why don't you get another one?"

"You know what would make this afternoon even *more* festive?" Wallace said, walking up to Bev. "Ida tells us you've got some spices at the ready. Might we be so lucky as to get some wassail?"

"Unfortunately, the spices must be saved for the Witzels' party," Bev said, not wanting to give the cleric more reason to drink. "But if you're still around when it happens, you're most welcome to have some."

His face fell. "That's a shame."

"It's worth the wait, trust me," Ida said. "The Witzels have been having their solstice party every year for at least the past century. It's our chance to say thank you to the local farmers and community for supporting the business. We're glad we can reclaim our spot at the Weary Dragon this year. Bev makes the best food, and that wassail is something to behold!"

"After several days of eating the food, I have to agree," he said. "You've certainly been blessed, Bev."

"I don't know about that," Bev said. "It's hard to go wrong with meat, potatoes, and bread."

Wallace chuckled as he walked toward the tree with more baubles.

Ida turned to the tree, sighing happily. "You know, I don't think I've felt festive until this moment. Thank you for letting me put up decorations. It really made me happy." She sighed and lowered her voice. "Now if we can only figure out who's trying to blackmail us, and why…then I'll really be in the holiday spirit." She bit her lip. "Was Rustin useless?"

"Yes, but I'm glad I spoke with him. I think mention of soldiers nearby might goad him into leaving his house," Bev said, smiling. "What have you learned from the folks here?"

"Nothing except that your clergyman likes to party," Ida said. "He all but cornered me the moment I walked inside." She nodded toward Abigail, who was keeping a much closer eye on her boys. "She seems nice, but she's about to snap from tension, I think. Unsure about her husband."

"Anyone else been around? Did you see the mystery man in room five?" Bev asked.

She shook her head. "No, the only people I've seen are the ones in this room. And like I said, Wallace wanted to talk my ear off the moment he saw me and Vel carrying in solstice decorations. Everyone seems really nice. Not like they're trying to blackmail us."

"Well, people can be funny," Bev said, watching the room for a moment.

"Are you going to visit Grant?"

She nodded. "Not today. In the morning. I've done enough walking for one afternoon. And I still have to get dinner ready."

Ida surveyed the tree, tilting her head. "You know, I think I've got some things we could hang above the mantel to really make that sparkle, too. Vel should be done with your order, so I'll bring both back—"

"Just be careful who sees you," Bev said. "Maybe come in through the kitchen."

Ida paused, glancing around the room as if she suddenly remembered *why* they were being blackmailed. "The sooner we figure this out, the happier I'll be."

CHAPTER NINE

Another night of Collin's playing, another morning when the snow remained stubbornly on the ground—but at least it didn't appear more had fallen in the night. Bev set to her usual chores quicker than normal. Her plan for the day was to check on Herman's goats, then "get lost" on the way back so she'd end up at Grant's house—and hope the farmer didn't see right through her.

Of course, she hadn't taken her suspicions off those staying with her at the inn, either. The Mysterious H, as she'd come to call him, did his usual storming down the stairs and out the door at daybreak before returning half an hour later, grumbling about the snow as he walked back upstairs. Bev hadn't seen the man eat in days, so she had to assume he was sneaking out at some point to find food. And maybe dropping threatening notes off at the Witzels'.

She heard noise out front and craned her neck to see who it was. "Morning, Allen."

Biscuit sat straight up, his nose pointed in the air as his tail began to wag just as the baker came into the kitchen carrying a basket full of flour discs, cheese, and dried meat. Biscuit, named for the delicacy, trotted over to meet Allen expectantly.

"Morning, Bev, Biscuit." Allen made up a sandwich for the laelaps, and Biscuit chomped down happily.

"Having trouble with the pastries this morning?" Bev asked. Allen had said once these were a backup plan when morning baking went awry.

"No, just trying to extend my stores a bit," he said. "I was hoping to travel to Middleburg to get more sugar before the solstice. This snow is something else, isn't it?"

Bev nodded. "Business okay over there?"

"Slow, of course. Not many people out and about, but Etheldra still wants me to bring a plate of sugar-coated pastries to the tea shop every morning. I think Earl's done a better job of keeping the streets clear near her house than over this way. The tea shop always seems busy."

"Well, that's good for Etheldra, anyway," Bev said, making herself a sandwich. "Listen, can I tell you something?"

"Anything."

"This isn't to be shared," Bev said, glancing around to make sure none of the guests were loitering. "But someone's been sending threatening notes to the Witzels."

Allen's jaw dropped, and his gaze narrowed angrily. "Who do I need to beat up? They're the nicest, the most—"

"No arguments here," Bev said with a chuckle. "I'm not quite sure. I have suspects, of course."

"Someone in the inn?"

"Maybe," Bev said. "Have you seen anyone loitering around the Witzels' back door lately?"

Allen's bakery was next door, so he'd have the best vantage. "Can't say that I see much of it, no. I did see the cadre of guests yesterday walking down the street. Plus, there's that one rude guy who always comes in to get himself a snack."

Bev started. "Rude guy?" Well, that certainly explained why the Mysterious H wasn't eating dinner. "Has he said anything to you?"

"Not a word except what he's buying," Allen said. "He comes first thing in the morning. Already came by, in fact. I don't see where he goes after he leaves town."

Bev glanced at the stairs. It certainly *sounded* like the Mysterious H in room five.

"Next time he comes in, I'll try to get a name."

"Hm." Bev rubbed her chin. Did that absolve or indict him? "Whatever you can glean from him, we'd appreciate it. I'm pulling on another thread today."

"What, exactly, are they threatening?" Allen asked.

"That's the thing: I'm not sure. The letters are vague. Current theory is someone's got information about Ida's magic."

"Understood," Allen said. His mother Fernley had also been a recipient of latent familial magic, though hers had been pobyd, which had accounted for the delicious things coming out of her kitchen. "So what's this thread you're pulling on?"

Bev explained what Max had said about Grant's cousin looking in the library at the Witzel family tree, which earned a chuckle from the baker. "Do you know about that whole blowup?"

Bev shook her head. "Ida said there was something about her great-grandfather and the butcher shop."

"From what I heard from my grandmother, the brothers got into an all-out brawl in the town square that had to be broken up by five people," Allen said.

"But you know how these town tales go."

Bev nodded. "I can't quite believe they'd want to extort Ida, but you never know. I'm headed out there today to talk with them."

"Good luck. I've been to the Klose Butcher Shops in Middleburg, and they tend to give you a side-eye when you tell them you're from Pigsend." He made a face. "Bad blood seems to run pretty deep there."

"Grant and I get on well, so hopefully that hasn't changed." Bev sighed. "I just hope I can get some answers before the solstice."

~

Bev finished her chores and dressed once again in her warmest clothes and socks that had been drying all night in the kitchen. She bade adieu to the guests, promising she'd give them a full report on the status of the roads when she returned, and headed west.

She passed Ramone's house, noticing the curl of smoke from the chimney and a few new statues on the front porch, but the artist didn't make an appearance. Bev would give them a few more days, perhaps until all the snow melted, then she'd swing by and apologize for offending them. If they were even still offended. They did tend to change moods like the weather.

She popped into Herman's house, finding the

goats to be well-fed and warm enough in the shed, before crossing the fields toward Grant's house.

The door opened before she reached the first step. "Bev? Is that you?" Grant walked out, rubbing his arms in the cold air.

"Grant?" Bev put her hand on her head, saying the only thing that came to her. "Well, I clearly took a wrong turn somewhere."

"What in the world are you doing all the way out here?" he asked.

"It's impossible to see where anything is out here in all this white," she said, hoping this ridiculous reason sounded plausible. "I was headed to Herman's house to check on his goats. He's out of town for the holiday."

"You're a far ways away from his place," Grant said. "Come in before you catch your death."

Well, that's one way to go about it.

Grant's house was warm and inviting, and Bev made sure to take off her sopping wet boots before continuing past the threshold. There was a small sitting area with a couch, two chairs by a roaring fire, and the smell of something sweet and spicy emanating from the kitchen.

"Whatcha got cooking in there?" Bev asked.

"Acorn bread," Grant said. "It should be about finished. You've got great timing."

Acorn bread was a laborious dish, but when

there was nothing else to do but sit around and wait for the snow to melt, it was a good way to pass the time with absolutely delicious results. Bev was more than happy to agree to a slice she didn't have to make herself—especially as it came with a special holiday blend of tea.

"I should take a wrong turn more often," Bev said with a smile as she sat in Grant's kitchen. She hadn't yet seen his cousin, and a small part of her hoped perhaps said cousin had already moved on.

"Hang on, let me tell Jasper it's ready," Grant said, rising from the table and walking to the stairs. "Jas? Food's ready."

"Do you have a guest?" Bev asked, hoping she sounded nonchalant.

"My cousin is in town from Middleburg," Grant said. "He's not the nicest of people, so I apologize in advance for his…attitude."

The man in question emerged from the staircase wearing a scowl. Bev could see the resemblance between the cousins, although his scowl was as different from Grant's affable smile as night and day. She greeted the cousin cordially and received a curt nod in return as he took a plate of bread and tea and sat across from Bev.

"So, Middleburg, hm?" Bev said, trying for conversation. "Do you come to Pigsend often?"

"I try to avoid distasteful places when I can,"

Jasper said, turning his nose up.

"Oh, ignore him," Grant said, waving his hand. "He's just mad he's stuck here instead of back home. But that's what happens when your mayor tries to cheat the Harvest Festival competition."

Bev cleared her throat. "What's that, now?"

"Jasper and I've had a running bet for the past decade," Grant said with a smirk to his scowling cousin. "Whoever brings home the most ribbons at the Pigsend Harvest Festival gets to host the other for the solstice. Well, it's the first time in our entire betting history that *Jasper* had to come here."

Jasper snorted. "And lucky me for getting snowed in this country bumpkin town the second day I'm here."

Bev sipped her tea. "Surely, there's something to like about Pigsend." She hesitated, deciding against letting him know Max had already alerted her to his presence. "The library is lovely."

"The only thing good about it is that there's a better archive of our family tree than in Middleburg," Jasper said. "Much better."

"A benefit of having fewer citizens, I'm sure," Bev said. "Are you a genealogy enthusiast?"

Jasper surveyed her for a long moment. "For some branches of our family tree. Others, of course, can be lost to time for all I care."

Bev itched to know if he was referring to the

Witzel butcher shop dispute but didn't feel ready to blurt it outright. "I think that's the case for a lot of families. One of the interesting things about Pigsend is how many folks are distantly related to one another." She paused. "Everyone except me, I assume."

"Yes, indeed," Grant said. "Did you know that we're related to the butchers? Well, Ida."

"I didn't," Bev said, hoping she didn't look like she was lying. "How are you connected?"

"Our great-grandfather was her great-grandfather's brother," Grant said, earning a scowl from Jasper.

"And that's the line that can be lost to time," Jasper said. "No-good thieves."

"My, I don't think that's..." Bev laughed a little nervously. "I wouldn't call Ida a thief."

"Not her, but her family sure was. The butcher shop was started by our great-great grandfather," Jasper said. "He left it to his boys, and *clearly* the older of the two should've taken ownership of it. But no... Ida's great-grandfather stole it out from under his brother and left us exiled to Middleburg."

"Now, Jasper, that's the story we heard from Nana," Grant said with a chuckle. "She about lost her mind when I told her I'd bought a plot of land here in Pigsend. Never once came to visit me."

"And nobody ever should!" Jasper said.

"Nothing to do in this town but steal from hardworking people."

"I'm sure Ida would disagree," Bev said. "You should pop in to see her sometime. They're doing their annual solstice party at the Weary Dragon. I'm sure you'd be welcome."

Grant nodded. "I've been invited, of course. The Witzels buy my pigs. But Jasper has made it clear he'd rather be dead than caught in their shop. Might get disowned by the rest of the family as I've been." He said it with a chuckle, and considering Jasper was here, *disowned* might be a stretch. "But I love my little plot of land. Been here nearly eight years now. I never did take to the butcher business like everyone else." Grant slapped his cousin on the shoulder, earning a grimace from the other man. "Jasper's going to take over soon, aren't you?"

He snorted. "That's the rumor, but you know how that goes."

Bev sipped her tea, getting a clearer picture of Jasper. He had no personal reason to be angry with Ida, but it had perhaps been ingrained in him by his family. He was on the cusp of inheriting what sounded like a nice business in the larger city of Middleburg. What motive did he have—other than pettiness—to send threatening notes to Ida?

Grant, too, could be a plausible suspect, using the threat of extortion to get the butchers to leave town so he could take over their business. But he'd admitted that he never "took" to the business.

Or did he say that to throw me off the trail?

Bev's inner voice was jumbled, and she hadn't a clue where to look or what to ask next. So much so that she missed what Grant was saying.

"Sorry, what was that?"

"I was asking what you planned to make for the Witzels' party. I assume they've hired you not just for your inn but also your cooking?" Grant asked. "Might we be so lucky to get some of that famed rosemary bread?"

"That's the plan," Bev said with a smile. "It really does depend on what they've got in stock. You know how it goes in the winter months."

"Too well," Grant said with a chuckle. "And this snow doesn't make it any easier."

"No," Bev sighed, "it doesn't."

~

Bev spent an hour talking farming and recounting the Harvest Festival tales with Grant before she decided it was time to make her escape. She hadn't found much of anything worth mentioning, and this whole trip seemed like yet another waste of her time. Jasper had excused himself within the first fifteen minutes of her visit, and she hadn't seen him since.

"Your cousin is itching to get back home, I take

it," Bev said as she and Grant trudged the length of his snowy fields toward the main street. "Surprised he honored your agreement as much as he dislikes this place."

"You know, I am, too," Grant said, rubbing the back of his head. "I honestly thought he'd back out and pay me the gold instead. Yet, here he is."

"Gold?" Bev asked.

He nodded. "It's either come spend the solstice or pay twenty gold coins." He shrugged. "I know he's a bit on the caustic side, but he really is a nice person once you get to know him."

Bev would have to take his word for it. "Thank you so much for your hospitality. I'm glad you don't seem to hold a grudge against Ida."

"Not at all," he said.

Bev hesitated, unsure if she wanted to ask her next question. But Grant had been in this town long enough that Ida's strength wouldn't be news to him.

"Listen, on the subject of family trees, I had a question about Ida..." Bev turned to him. "And her...well..."

"Unusual strength?" Grant chuckled. "Wherever she got *that* from, it certainly wasn't our side of the family. Though I'm sure it comes in handy for her."

Bev nodded. "Any ideas which it does come from?"

"Not particularly," Grant said. "Though I do

believe Etheldra Daws is related to her through her mother's side."

"E...Etheldra?" Bev blinked. The same pointed woman who ate nearly every night in Bev's inn? The owner of the tea shop? That Etheldra?

"I remember my Nana saying that Ida's grandfather was nuts for marrying into the Daws clan—they were 'weird,' in her words. I'd always chalked it up to the latent grudge, but..." He shrugged. "Maybe she knows where the magic came from?"

"Maybe." Or maybe she held another clue to the threatening letters. "Appreciate the chat, as always. I suppose I'll see you at the party, eh?"

"If I don't see you first!"

CHAPTER TEN

Bev didn't believe for one second that Etheldra Daws would send threatening letters to Ida and Vellora. The old woman was direct, a little cantankerous, but her tea shop was always busy with shoppers and sippers alike, and Bev couldn't see a scenario where she would even *want* gold from Ida.

But it was still a question—and she'd learned from Claude that no one was absolved of guilt until she'd made absolutely sure they had no ulterior motives.

So after a quick pop in at the inn, where she had the unfortunate task of telling her guests that the roads were still too snowy for them to leave, Bev checked on her bread, petted Biscuit, who was happy playing with the two little boys, and donned her things again.

"Going out so soon?" Bernie asked.

"I…uh…" Bev cleared her throat. "Running low on tea, so I'm headed to the local shop."

"Oh, I'd love to join you, if you don't mind," he said. "I've heard such wonderful things and…well, it's nice to stretch the legs."

Bev hadn't had a chance to get to know Bernie, so she readily accepted his offer and the two of them set off down the street. Some kind citizen had come through with a shovel again to make things a little easier, but the cold wind was brutal, and there were ice patches everywhere.

"I'd hoped things would be better by now," Bernie said, moving slowly to keep his balance.

"It's a strange year, that's for sure," Bev said.

"I worry about poor Estera. Hope she made it to her mother's house all right. We've been lucky it hasn't snowed any more, but it hasn't been exactly pleasant." He glanced at Bev, almost a bit eagerly. "What got her so intent on leaving? Do you know?"

Bev shook her head. "Nope. But I also hope she made it safely to wherever she was going."

"She really didn't say a word to you about—"

"So, you're from the south? What brings you up here?" Bev said, eager to get off the subject of Estera.

"Oh, this and that," he said. "I'm a nomadic sort of man. Never stay in one spot for too long—unless, of course, I'm snowed in!" He chuckled. "I fell into some nice work with a scholar in Sheepsburg who needed an extra pair of hands to do their annual accounting. Paid me handsomely and set me up for at least another month of lackadaisical travel."

"You travel from town to town in search of work, then?" Bev asked. "You know, our local archivist Max was telling me his nephew was unable to make it this year to help him with the accounting. If you get bored, you might find some work with him."

He nodded with a bit of a nervous laugh. "I find, actually, that if I don't *have* to work, I don't really *want* to. Part of my nomadic spirit, you know."

To not *have* to work? "I've never known such a life."

"No? Surely, you had some days in your childhood where you could lie in a field of flowers and watch the clouds go by?"

"If I did, I don't remember them," Bev said, briefly explaining her origin story. "So ever since I arrived here, I've been working at the inn. But the work gives me purpose and a reason to get up in the morning. Plus, I get to chat with interesting folks like yourself."

"I don't know," Bernie said with a shake of his head. "You do work awfully hard. You should give the leisurely life a try once in a while."

Bev nodded as they came into the town square. "It gets pretty quiet after the solstice. Everything really shuts down, and people stay in their houses. But I always get a guest or two and dinner needs making for those in town who want a hot meal. Plus, there's the mule and dog to tend to, and if I don't keep up with the floors and windows, they get filthy…" Bev rattled off more of her daily chores, earning a groan from Bernie.

"You should hire help," he said. "At one gold piece a night, you certainly can afford it."

"Sometimes," Bev said. "But I like having ownership of the place. I know things get done right the first time."

"Young Collin isn't cleaning up to your standards?" he said with a chuckle.

Bev snorted. After several nights of decent work, this morning she'd found the kitchen not quite as clean as she'd hoped. "If he wants a warm bed, he's got to pull his weight. Or cough up some gold."

"He's asking the wrong people," Bernie said. "Keeps sniffing around the cleric for a tip, but everyone knows the clergy have no money. Now, if he came to me, I'm sure I could find something for him to do for me."

"Like what?"

"Oh…" He tapped his finger to his chin. "Well, I'm sure I'd think of something."

Bev smiled as they came into the main square. The tea shop was beyond the schoolhouse, which was closed for the winter. It was a quaint little building that sometimes had tables outside. People came to buy their tea in bulk for their morning cuppa, but also to enjoy the day's special brew. Bev was especially fond of the solstice blend that made its appearance around this time.

Inside, the small tea room was warm and inviting, with a roaring fire in the hearth and five tables situated around the room. There were a couple of folks sipping on tea and talking, including Allen and his would-be girlfriend Vicky at one table, and the Silvers, Freddie and Hans, who seemed to be sharing one of Allen's sugar-coated pastries and staring lovingly into each other's eyes, at another.

At the counter, Shasta Brewer was helping a customer with a large order, pulling canisters off the shelf and scooping them into small bags. When the customer turned, Bev recognized Mayor Jo Hendry all bundled up in a smart tailored coat and perfectly clean boots that defied logic.

"And the solstice blend, too," she said before noticing Bev and Bernie standing behind her. "Oh, good morning. Surprised to see you out and about in this nasty weather."

"Likewise," Bev said with a nod. "Mayor Hendry, this is Bernie Shaffer. He's staying at the inn."

"Longer than I'd hoped," he said, eyeing her for a minute before brightening. "You're the mayor, Bev said? You've got a lovely town here. I'm sure it's much prettier in the spring."

"Much," Hendry said, taking the bags of loose-leaf tea from Shasta. "Bev, things all right at the inn?"

Bev hesitated, wondering if she should mention the Witzels' letters. "Things are lovely."

"Oh good, because Rustin said you'd stopped in to visit him yesterday," she said, running a long nail around her perfectly shaped lips.

What Rustin had told Hendry was anyone's guess, but Bev didn't want to discuss it in front of Bernie. "Oh, yes. Just wanted to check in with something about the Witzels' annual holiday party. I assume we'll be seeing you?"

"I'll try to make an appearance," she said with a long sigh. "But even getting out the door is so much trouble. We're lucky folks have taken it upon themselves to shovel some of the streets."

"No thanks to our hibernating mayor." Etheldra's grainy voice echoed from the stairwell behind them. Although she was old, Etheldra took the stairs sprightly, crossing the room to stand behind the counter with Shasta. "First time I've seen you out and about lately. Hope you've thanked Earl for doing your job."

"I certainly will if I see him." The mayor wrapped herself up in her scarf and swept out the door without another word.

Shasta shared a nervous look with Bev, while Etheldra glared at the door for a moment before turning her ire onto the next customers in line.

"What are you doing here?" she barked at Bev. "Here to convince me to return to dinner at the inn? Well, not until that loudmouth bard is gone."

"No, of course not," Bev said. "I needed to get a refill on some tea for the inn."

"You got a refill last week."

Bev forced a smile as they stared at each other in silence.

"I'd like to get a cup of this solstice blend," Bernie said, stepping forward. "It smells delicious."

"I'll get right on that," Shasta said. "Come with me. Would you like any honey or sugar?"

The two left Bev and Etheldra staring at each other across the counter. The other woman sniffed. "Now why are you really here?"

"I had a couple of questions for you, if you've got a moment," Bev said.

"Ask."

"Well, perhaps we could go somewhere a bit less crowded?"

She sighed. "Then why didn't you say so?"

Bev followed Etheldra out into what was usually a lush garden with hanging tree limbs overhead and more tables for sitting and enjoying the day. Now, however, it was covered in snow like everything else. Bev shivered for a moment, even though she still wore her cloak, but it was probably more due to Etheldra's frosty glare.

"Well? What is it?"

Bev decided it was better to ask the questions than beat around the bush. "You're related to Ida Witzel, aren't you?"

"Of course. Her grandmother was my first cousin. Why?"

"Well, I'm trying to figure out…" Bev cleared her throat. "Someone's been sending the Witzels threatening letters. Not quite sure what they're really after, but the letters indicate they want gold. I wanted to know if you had any idea who might be sending them?"

"Probably those dastardly Kloses," Etheldra said. "You know one of the Middleburg scum is in town? I try to avoid them if I can."

Bev cleared her throat. "But you're not related to them, right?"

"No, I just don't like them. That Grant is too nice for his own good."

"I see." She shifted. "I wonder if the letters have anything to do with Ida's strength."

"Don't be daft, of course they do," she said. "That or her wife's wartime service. Have you looked into that at all?"

Bev shook her head. "Vellora thinks it's Ida that they're trying to blackmail."

"Of course she does. Doesn't want to be blamed for the problems. I'd do the same thing."

They were getting off course. "I guess... Do you have any clue where this super strength came from? The Kloses don't believe it's from their line. But they thought it might...um. Might have come from the Daws side. Do you know anything about dryads?"

Etheldra adjusted her cloak. "Of course I do. Woodland nymphs. They say that a long time ago there was a nymph in the family line, but we all thought it was poppycock until Ida started carrying pigs three times her size when she was a little girl."

"Why do you think her parents didn't say anything?"

"Well, what's there to say?" Etheldra barked. "She's got curly hair, and she can lift heavy things. It's just another interesting fact about her." She paused. "Well, it was until that damn queen came into power. If you ask me, she ruined just about everything."

Bev nodded. "We think whoever's blackmailing the Witzels is planning to take what they know to the soldiers stationed to the north. Once the snow melts, of course. But it's got them spooked. Any insight you could give me…"

"Another mystery to solve, eh, Bev?" The woman eyed her. "You know you might as well add 'super sleuth' to your title at the inn."

"Just trying to help out my friends," Bev said.

"I'd start by investigating those no-good Kloses," Etheldra said. "You know, I hear that their business is failing. The latest generation seems to be mucking things up good."

Bev frowned. "Really? I hadn't heard that."

"Surprised Ida hasn't mentioned it, all the bad blood between them." She chuckled. "Would make a pretty decent motive, if you ask me." She adjusted her cloak. "Now if you'll excuse me, I must be getting back to work."

Bev returned to the tea shop where Bernie was seated at the table with someone who had his back to Bev. Bernie motioned for her to join them, and as Bev rounded the table, she stopped short.

A uniformed queen's soldier.

"Bev, this is Henry Markum," Bernie said.

"Hello," the soldier said, nodding at Bev.

"Bev," she replied, taking the empty third seat and watching him warily. "Traveling into town?"

"No, I was doing a quick inspection," he said, bringing the teacup to his lips. From his tone, he, like Estera, didn't want to say where he was coming from. "This tea is quite good."

"I agree," Bev said, wondering if Bernie might've gotten more out of the soldier. "Are you in need of a room tonight? We have one left—"

"No. I'm headed back as soon as I thaw myself."

"Back to where?" Bev asked.

"The rest of my regiment," he said, putting the empty teacup down. "I must be getting going. Thank you for the seat and the cuppa."

"Oh, regiment?" Bev said, hoping she sounded innocent. "Then you must know Estera Pongo."

He stopped. "I do."

"She was staying at my inn recently," Bev said. "Left to go home, she said. She'd thought her regiment had moved on, but it appears you're still nearby."

"Indeed." He nodded. "Good day."

With that, he left without another word.

"Hello and goodbye," Bev said, watching him with a frown. "Did he happen to say where he was staying? I can't imagine he's walking all the way to Middleburg in this weather."

"No, I got about as much information out of him as you did," he said with a chuckle. "I like queen's soldiers, you know? They've always got some good story to share about their journeys across this country. Though normally, they're much chattier when you buy them a cup of tea."

"Did he say what he was inspecting?" Bev asked, glancing out the window. The soldier was still visible, struggling through the high snowbanks farther out of town.

"The only thing in town worth inspecting is the snow," Bernie said. "You know, maybe he suspects someone's cast a spell and made it snow. The quiet ones tend to be more interested in magic."

Bev could attest to that. "I should've asked if he worked for Karolina Hunter. She passed through town a few months ago and had the same…uh… type of personality. Very interested in finding magic, much to the detriment of the town, I might add."

"Oh, well…" He nodded, as if this wasn't a surprise to him. "Did she find anything?"

Bev thought of the two amulet pieces buried in several inches of snow and dirt. "No, can't say she did. But we're certainly keeping our eyes open for any magical nonsense."

~

Bernie had brought a book to read and wasn't eager to get back out in the snow, so Bev donned her heavy cloak and trudged back to the Weary Dragon by herself. She still had a few chores left to do, not to mention putting in her meat order for the day.

She slowed as the Witzel Butchery came into view and chewed her lip. Ida and Vellora needed to know a soldier had been in town, albeit briefly, and Bev wanted to ask them about Etheldra, the Kloses, and what they knew of Ida's family tree.

Up ahead, Ida came trudging through the snow, sans cloak or coat, holding a letter as her breath pooled around her face, and Bev's heart sank.

"Another one?" Bev asked.

The longer you wait, the worse it'll be.
A hundred gold coins. Tonight. Or else.

CHAPTER ELEVEN

"Still no indication who they're talking about, right?" Bev looked between the two of them. "Vellora, you're *sure* it's not you?"

"I'm very sure," she said with a frown. "It has to be Ida's magic. What could someone have on me?"

Bev turned the letter over, sitting in the Witzels' living room near the fire. Ida was pacing the room, and Vellora was standing over the other chair, gripping it tightly. The living room itself was well-loved, with a matching sofa across from the two chairs, a low table filled with books, and some charcoal sketches Ida had drawn. There were paintings on nearly every wall, including one that appeared to be of Ida's parents when Ida was a little girl. She and her father seemed to share many features, including a dazzling smile. There wasn't much of Vellora in this room, but perhaps that was how the other butcher liked it.

Bev glanced at Vellora, Etheldra's warning about her past echoing in her ears. "I'm trying to look at all possible angles. It could very well be Ida's magic they're talking about, but if there's something from your...wartime past that you aren't telling us..."

The butcher's face darkened considerably, and although she looked like she was ready to break the chair in half, she took several calming breaths. "I swear, on my wife's beautiful heart, that I have nothing to hide."

"Fair enough," Bev said, holding up her hands in surrender. "So it was just this letter? Nothing else?"

"That's it," Ida said, pointing to the letter in Bev's hand. "Just like the others. No detail, no sign of who left it there."

"What time was it left?" Bev asked.

The two butchers shared a look. "I found it around nine this morning."

When Bev was at Grant's house, not watching the comings and goings at the inn. "And no sign of who dropped it off?"

Vellora shook her head. "It was just there."

"Tell me you've found something," Ida said. "Because otherwise, I might lose my mind."

Bev wished she had more to tell. "I went out to Grant's this morning to talk with him about his cousin. Jasper says he lost a bet with Grant then got stuck with all the snow. But something's a bit fishy about all of it." She tilted her head. "Etheldra Daws tells me that their business is in trouble in Middleburg."

"It is?" Vellora said, looking at Ida, who nodded.

"I'd heard that."

Vellora threw her hands in the air. "You did?"

She lifted a shoulder. "You hear things from farmers who live closer to Middleburg. A lot of them told me they stopped selling to the Kloses after they started not paying as much. Not sure why they decided to change their prices, but it turned a lot of the farmers off."

"You didn't think to mention that to Bev?" Vellora asked. "They *could* be behind these letters if they're looking for money!"

Ida made a flustered noise. "Well, I don't... I mean, I didn't think it was pertinent. Because—"

"I have to agree," Bev said, stepping in to save Ida. "They're asking for a hundred gold coins. That's not enough to save a failing business."

"Exactly," Ida said. "Besides that, the Witzel bad blood... It's been ages since anyone's actually cared.

Now I feel like it's all for show."

"Jasper certainly didn't act like it was," Bev said. "But I can't really pin him here because he hasn't been in town since the snow fell."

"He could be dropping off the letters and running," Vellora suggested.

"What else have you found?" Ida asked Bev.

"Allen says there's a mysterious stranger who comes in first thing in the morning, buys a pastry, then heads north. Not sure if that's the cantankerous guest in room five or someone else." Bev paused. "Today, I was in the tea shop with Bernie, one of the guests. He's certainly still on the list. Seems nice enough, but not one for working hard, if you get my drift." Bev cleared her throat. "More importantly, a queen's soldier came in."

The two butchers sobered. "Really?" Ida said.

"What are they after?"

"He didn't say, which was concerning, of course," Bev said. "But more so is the worry… He said he was returning to his regiment after doing *an inspection*, whatever that means. But the regiment can't be that far if he's able to come down to Pigsend."

"Is it Estera's regiment?" Ida asked.

Bev nodded and the butchers went silent for a moment, the only sound the crackling fire.

"I'll keep digging," Bev said.

Downstairs, the bell tinkled, signaling someone had come in. Vellora made a noise as she turned toward the staircase. "I'll see who it is."

Ida crossed the room to sit in the chair across from Bev. "Surely, Bev, you've got something more concrete?"

"I know I've been roped into these things a few times, but I'm no expert," Bev said, taking her hand.

"We have a solstice party in three days," Ida said, more to herself. "We've already started preparing all the meat, and I'm *not* letting that go to waste. Whoever this person is…we're not going to let them win."

"Too right you are," Bev said with a firm nod. "I'll return to the inn and keep asking questions until I find out who's behind all this." She began counting off the guests in her head. "Bernie, of course, but he's not in need of money, so he says. Collin the bard is *definitely* in need of money and doesn't seem to have any skills to earn it other than playing his lute. The clergy couple…Wallace is something of a drunk and Paul a cheapskate, so they could be involved. Byron and Abigail, the couple with the kids, they don't seem to be in need of money—"

"You really suspect them?" Ida asked with a chuckle. "Are they having the two little boys deliver the blackmail notes?"

"You never know." Bev smiled. "Plus, the Kloses still aren't off the hook. And Etheldra—"

"What about me?"

Ida and Bev looked up as the old woman ascended the stairs, with a very confused Vellora following. Etheldra carried a thick book in her arms and didn't seem surprised to see Bev there.

"Etheldra, what can we do for you?" Ida asked, rising slowly.

"It's come to my attention that Ida doesn't know where her magic comes from. And that you're being blackmailed."

Ida and Vellora's gaze shifted to Bev, and she held up her hands. "What? It's not a surprise to Etheldra that Ida's strong. She's been in town her whole life."

"But the blackmail, Bev," Ida said.

"Oh, pish-posh, who am I going to tell?" Etheldra bristled. "Look, would you like to know the source of your magic or not?"

Ida chewed her lip. "Is it…bad?"

"Of course not. Why would it be?"

"Well, I don't know if it's on the queen's approved list of magical creatures," Ida said, rubbing her hands together. "And if I find out—"

"You've got it whether you know it or not. And no, it's not on the so-called *official list*, but that hasn't stopped you from throwing cow carcasses over your shoulder, has it?"

"I suppose not…"

"Then let's dive in."

~

Vellora put on a kettle, and the four of them settled around the Witzels' dining room table. It was a bit cramped, especially with Vellora, but somewhat cozy.

"These scones are a bit dry," Etheldra said, tapping them on the table. "Did you get them from Mackey last week?"

"I did," Ida said, her cheeks darkening. "Wasn't expecting company."

"You should always expect company, especially in this town," Etheldra said, flipping open the book. "Now, how much do you know about your magic?"

"N-nothing," Ida said, sharing a bewildered look with Vellora. "Just that I have it."

"Bit of a miracle that you do," Etheldra said.

"Why's that?"

"Well, because the magic's been all but dead in our family tree for generations," Etheldra replied. "At least two hundred years since anyone's had anything more than a shadow. You've got full-blown magic, child."

"What kind of magic is it?" Ida asked. "Is it the dryad?"

"That Renault or Claude fellow was on the

money there," Etheldra said with a dark chuckle. "Should've hung around a little bit longer, might've found some more so-called *hidden* magic right under his nose."

"What's a dryad anyway?" Bev asked. "I…uh… have heard it's something like a nymph."

Etheldra cast a long, scrutinizing look at Bev before nodding and opening the book. "Yes, they're part of the same family. Now, of course, *true* dryads get their magic from a connection with oak trees, but as we started marrying non-magical humans, diluting the line more until the magic was no longer there for most of us. But *every* so often, the right combination of lines come together, and the magic reappears." She flipped to a large family tree. "This is my second cousin once removed on my father's side. He was able to sense the weather. And over here." She pointed a bit farther up. "My grandmother's great-aunt was said to be able to locate fish by putting her finger in the water."

"But not strength," Ida said.

"As I said, the magic is there, but how it presents itself comes from the other side—in this case, your father. I wouldn't be surprised if somewhere in his family tree, there was some creature with strength."

Ida nodded, looking a bit shell-shocked. "So that's it, then. I'm a…dryad."

"Descended from one, at least," Etheldra said with a sniff, but then she softened, putting her hand over Ida's. "I'm sorry I didn't tell you sooner. Never thought it needed explanation, you know? Your folks felt you were happier believing you were blessed with good muscles and left it at that."

"You talked to them about this?" Ida asked.

"Not in so many words."

"Do you have any magic?" Vellora asked.

Etheldra took a long look at her before nodding. "Much like the rest of the family, it's not as obvious, but I believe it's there. I've always had a preternatural way of combining herbs and spices for teas, knowing exactly how to put them together to make the best blend. Even so far as knowing when there's a substandard harvest for the year. It's part of why my tea shop has done so well these past fifty years." She cast her dark gaze onto Bev and quirked a brow. "Bev, I'm sure you can relate."

"I don't have magic," Bev said, holding up her hands. "The herb garden just…does well on its own. There's probably magic in the ground I don't know about."

Etheldra didn't break her stare for a few moments then shrugged. "If you say so."

"I don't understand," Vellora said. "How is knowing what she is going to help her?"

"Well, *if* these letters are because of your magic,

and not, as I suspect, your *wife's* past," she cast a dirty glare at Vellora, who returned it with gusto, "then it's helpful to be prepared. I've heard tales of people in other cities who have this sort of latent magic getting accused of eating the wrong sort of magical potion or stealing magic from someone else. If you're able to prove magic this way, you stand a chance of beating charges of illegal magical use."

"I know people who've been taken away for magic, though," Vellora said. "People like Ida."

"Well, see, if Ida was a full dryad, we'd have a problem. But she can merely show that her magic is a fluke, a passing fancy, and not the kind the queen's really concerned about…" She bristled. "In any case, there's nothing anyone can do right now. It's not as if there's a contingent of soldiers staying nearby."

Bev, Ida, and Vellora shared a nervous look, all thinking the same thing.

"*Is* there a contingent of soldiers staying nearby?" Etheldra asked.

"Yes, sort of," Bev said. "There was a soldier at your tea shop today. He said he was returning to his regiment after inspecting the town."

"Hmph." She made a face. "He can inspect all he wants. Wouldn't be the first queen's soldier sniffing in my herbs for magic. That Karolina Hunter was in my tea shop almost every day."

"I didn't realize—" Bev started, but Etheldra

waved her off.

"You know as well as I do that the soldiers this far out tend to have their own agendas and rules based on their whims. I was honestly surprised that Claude fellow didn't snap you up, Ida, what with how you flaunt your strength all over the place. But he didn't seem to think you were worth worrying over. Neither did Karolina Hunter. Can I be sure others would feel the same way? No. But it's better to be prepared anyway."

"And we still don't know who's sending us these letters," Vellora said.

"Clearly, it's someone across the street at the inn," Etheldra said. "Bev, you're good at this sort of investigating thing now. Why don't you go ask the guests at your inn what secrets they're hiding?"

"It's not as if they're coming out and talking with me," Bev said with a chuckle. When no one joined her, she added, "Short of threatening them— which we are *not* doing, Vellora—I don't know how else to get them to open up to me."

"Follow them when they leave," Etheldra said, as if it were obvious. "Search their rooms for letters and ink."

"I'm not breaking their trust like that," Bev said. "They're nice folks and most likely innocent of blackmail. But I will redouble my efforts to get to know them better. After all," she glanced out the window where snow was threatening again, "it doesn't look like they're going anywhere any time soon."

"Fine," Etheldra said, rising and closing the book behind her. "I suppose I'll have to handle things myself."

"What does that mean?" Bev asked as the old woman made her way toward the stairs.

"You'll just have to find out," Ida replied with a half-shrug as Etheldra disappeared down the stairs.

CHAPTER TWELVE

Etheldra's mysterious warning aside, Bev did need to get back to the inn to check on things and start dinner. As she crossed the snowy street, she conceded she was farther from the truth than ever, but she resolved to do her best to get to know each of her guests better.

But all that went out the window when she pushed open the front door to the inn to absolute chaos.

The boys were chasing a barking Biscuit while screaming and being chased by their father, and the baby was crying in his mother's arms as she scolded both the boys and her husband for running too much. Wallace had already gotten into the ale, and his husband Paul seemed to be mid-argument with Collin, who had his lute in his hand. Bernie was in the corner, looking disgruntled by all the noise and holding his book to his chest. And, of course, the Mysterious H was nowhere to be seen.

Bev put her fingers to her lips and whistled loudly. The boys and dog stopped running, the baby stopped crying, the two men stopped arguing, and all eyes swept to Bev.

"That's better," she said. "I do apologize for being gone most of the day, but we can't have the inn descending into madness." She pointed to Biscuit. "You, to the kitchen." She pointed to the boys. "You two, sit down by the fire and let your father deal with you." She turned to Wallace. "You, no more ale this evening. You've had more than you've paid for, and if you don't stop, I'll have nothing for the solstice party in three days." She turned to Paul and Collin. "And as for you two, what in the world could be your problem?"

"He dared ask me to *pay* for the infernal music he's been playing," Paul said.

"I've been playing for hours, whatever his husband wanted," Collin said. "And I deserve compensation for my work."

"Then you should've presented those terms up front," Paul replied haughtily. "Because I surely would've enjoyed the last few nights without having to listen to your off-tune voice and poorly played instrument."

Collin's expression darkened, and Bev stepped between them to prevent the situation from escalating. "Collin, Paul is right. If you wanted to be paid for your playing, you should've said something *before* you started playing. Paul, if you don't like the music, go upstairs."

"But I can *hear* it—"

"I don't care. Both of you are about to be sent to your rooms without any supper if you don't cut it out," Bev snapped. "I'm sorry we're all stuck here another night, but it's no excuse for everyone losing their minds. Now can I ask the two of you to behave while I finish getting dinner ready?"

They glared daggers at one another but nodded. Paul turned to grab his inebriated husband by the shoulder and practically dragged him upstairs while Collin retreated to the corner and started tuning his lute, and nearly everyone in the room looked ready to break the darn thing in half.

"Collin," Bev said lightly. "Why don't you come help me with dinner? We'll say that's your payment for this evening, huh?"

In truth, Bev didn't need help with dinner, but having Collin peel potatoes was an efficient way to keep him from causing more problems in the main room and also to have a bit of a chat with him. Of all the suspects, he certainly had the most to gain from blackmailing the butchers—but Bev didn't know *how* desperate he was for gold.

"I hate peeling potatoes," he whined, sitting on Bev's stool and grabbing the nearest spud. "Are you sure the roads are impossible to travel on? Bernie said a soldier came and went. Estera left."

Bev watched his face carefully. "No one's keeping you here, Collin. If you'd like to try your luck, you can. Kaiser Tuckey's house isn't *that* far away."

He sighed. "You know, this gig was supposed to set me up for a few months. At least through the winter."

"You and Bernie have the same mindset, it seems," Bev said. "Have you had a chance to talk much with him?"

"Oh, yes. We've had a lot of time since there's not much else to do," he said. "We've been to many of the same towns. He's about as well-traveled as I am, though his line of work seems a bit more haphazard."

At least Bernie's story is consistent.

"He was telling me the same. I told him if he was looking for some money, he should check in with the librarian. He's lacking his usual end-of-year help."

Collin spun around. "He is? Do you think I could help him? It might be less exhausting than dishes or peeling potatoes."

Bev chuckled. "I'm sure you could ask. Can't say it would pay much, but it might get you a night or two off."

"Oh, the dream." He sighed.

"You know," Bev began slowly, "I'm not a bard or in the music business at all. Can't carry a tune to save my life. But…" She eyed him. "I would think a man like yourself would at least *ask* people to pay before striking up a tune."

"Typically, I start playing, people offer suggestions, and at the end of the night, they tip handsomely for my efforts," he said. "But I supposed I should've known the cleric and his husband were stingy."

"Yes, they seem pretty consistent in that arena," Bev said. "I think Paul is about to make his husband join you in the kitchen."

"Would be better than all the drinking he does," Collin said. "I've never seen a man put away as much ale as him."

"Me neither." And Bev had seen some people drink some ale. "So…is music the only thing you do for a living? It seems like a bit of a low-income job."

"When you're stuck at an inn, it can be," he

said. "But you play a little bit here and there, hoping a wealthy benefactor will hear your music and hire you to play a gig at their house. Sometimes, it's a birthday party. Sometimes, it's the solstice. Sometimes, it's a weekday, and they want to show off to their friends. But you can get fifty gold pieces for a few hours of playing. Do that enough times, and you don't have to work that much."

"Sounds nice," Bev said. "Are you at that point yet?"

"Kaiser Tuckey was my first big gig," he said with a sigh. "And he's got a lot of rich friends who were going to be at his house. But…" He shook his head. "Maybe it wasn't meant to be."

"Any other prospects to make you money?" Bev asked. Sure, it was a pointed question, and she doubted he'd come right out and say, "I'm blackmailing your neighbors," but it was late, and she was running out of steam.

"Sounds like the librarian might be my best bet at this point," he said, sadly. "Or I could return home and go to work for my father in the tannery. I'm sure he would have a great laugh at my failure. Never wanted me to play an instrument. Thought it was a waste of time." He glared at the ceiling. "You know, *Paul* reminds me a lot of him. Judgmental and rude."

Bev nodded, hoping that by staying silent, he

might offer more than he was.

"But really, I should be charging the guy in room five more money," he said with a sigh.

"Room five?" Bev turned to him. "What are you doing for him?"

"Well, he gives me a quarter of a silver to bring him a bowl of dinner after everyone goes to bed," he said. "Started last night, but I'm sure he'll want the same tonight."

That certainly explained the extra bowl she'd found this morning. "I see. Do you know why he doesn't want to come down and eat with everyone else?"

"Haven't a clue. Maybe he's afraid of people, or maybe he doesn't like kids." He shrugged. "Either way, I'm slowly working my way up to a full silver."

"Collin, love," Bev said, putting her hand on his shoulder, "you *really* should be charging people more. Or getting the money up front, at least. A quarter of a silver is hardly anything. Why not charge him a whole silver? Then you won't have to do dishes."

The young man nodded as if the idea hadn't occurred to him at all. "You think he'd pay?"

"I think that if he wants to remain anonymous, he'll pay any price you tell him," Bev said. "So in this case, you have the upper hand."

"Oh." He blinked, mulling over the idea. "You

know, that kind of makes sense."

Bev squeezed his shoulder, a little sorry for him.

"Wish I'd thought of that before I started doing all this work," Collin said, looking down at the stack of potatoes he was working his way through. "Maybe I should be a bit smarter about these things. My dad was right, I guess."

She watched him, torn between feeling awful for him and wondering if this was another brilliant show meant to hide his true intentions. Perhaps he secretly *loved* cleaning and peeling potatoes and was pretending to slough his way through it to keep her from suspecting him. And played until the wee hours of the morning because he enjoyed it, not because he expected to get paid. It was all so very plausible.

"What else did Bernie say about that soldier?" Bev asked, after a long pause.

"Just that he bought him a cuppa, and the soldier left shortly afterward," Collin said. "Said he was in Estera's regiment."

Bev started. To her knowledge, Estera had only divulged her soldier status to Bev. "Oh? She told you she was a soldier?"

Collin nodded. "First night we were here. I was walking by her room as she was unpacking—had the door open. Saw the soldier uniform and asked her about it. She told me she was a part of a group looking for illegal magic and that she was glad she wasn't with them, as they were sleeping in tents in an empty field north of here."

Bev carefully ran her knife through the meat, processing what he'd said. Not just soldiers— soldiers looking for *illegal magic*. Concerning to say the least. "I see."

"Guess it makes sense one of them would venture into town looking for something warm after all this snow." He shivered. "Glad I never took up with the queen's service. Too much time spent outdoors and harassing people."

"It's not all bad, I hear," Bev said, hoping for mild conversation about it. "So…Estera really told you all that? She didn't even want to say what she did to me."

"To be honest, I think she was hoping for… Well, you know, I have that effect on women." Collin glanced at Bev. "Er…*some* women. Young women. They see the lute, and they take a shine to me."

"And I'm sure you've never used that to your advantage," Bev said with a knowing look.

"In what way?" Collin asked.

If he was a brilliant mastermind, he was hiding it well, because the blank stare he gave her was awfully convincing.

"So, who else knows that Estera's a soldier?" Bev

asked. That might be the clue she was looking for to narrow the suspects.

"Oh, well, probably everyone now," Collin said with a small laugh. "When she hightailed it out of the inn after that butcher harassed her, I told the folks here I thought the butcher was a kingside soldier looking for revenge."

Bev winced. That certainly didn't help things at all. "I see. She isn't, by the way. Just...a case of mistaken identity."

"If you say so." Collin hopped off the stool. "Anything else you want me to do?"

Bev inspected the potatoes and found half of them still contained scraps of skin. But she needed some time to think about what he'd said.

"Look, why don't you go upstairs and negotiate a new price for bringing him dinner?" she said. "Make sure you charge him what you deserve this time."

"What if he doesn't pay?" Collin said.

"Then bring the stew back to me, and we'll give it to Biscuit," Bev said, earning a tail wag from the dog at her feet. "And if the Mysterious H wants to eat, he'll have to come down himself."

Bev made quick work of the unfinished potatoes, her mind engrossed in thought. So everyone at the inn knew that Estera was a soldier—

and not just any soldier, but part of a special magic-hunting regiment camped out to the north of here. Vellora had been right. The blackmailer knew far more than they did.

But the timeline didn't quite make sense. Estera had arrived before the first note, and Vellora had threatened her before the second note. Had Collin met Estera, discovered she was a magical hunter, seen Ida carry in the tree with her magic, and devised the whole plan on a whim—maybe once the snow fell and his chances of a big gig with Kaiser Tuckey went up in smoke?

As much as she wanted to believe it, she was having a hard time. Collin was either an incredible actor or completely innocent.

"Biscuit," Bev muttered to the laelaps at her feet, begging for a scrap of potato skin. "What do we think about Collin?"

He tilted his head, almost curious.

"I mean, is he thick or do we think he's capable of blackmail?" Bev asked.

Biscuit had no answer.

She finished cooking dinner, plated it up, and brought it out to the front room with a fake smile on her face. The crowd was subdued—Wallace seemed to have sobered up enough to at least look sheepish for his behavior—as they queued up to serve themselves.

"Did you get the coin from room five?" Bev asked Collin as he passed by.

"Oh, yes, sorry." He reached into his pocket and handed Bev two silvers. "And I managed to get him to pay me a full silver to bring him dinner, too!"

"Save this one," Bev said, handing it back to him. "You've already worked off your room tonight."

"Is that option available to *all* of us?" Paul asked, giving the musician a once-over.

"Of course," Bev said. "I've always got chores that need doing. Just say the word, and you're welcome to join me in the stables to muck the stalls or peel potatoes or scrub dishes."

Paul made a face as if *none* of those things appealed to him and slapped down a silver before walking off to sit at one of the empty tables. Wallace said nothing and joined him.

"I think we'd rather pay the coin if we have it," Bernie said with a chuckle as he gave her his rent for the evening.

Bev itched to ask him more about the soldier, about Estera, but she kept her tongue. Best to do that one-on-one instead of in the open room, lest one of the other guests got suspicious.

Everyone was served, and Bev made herself a small plate to eat at her counter. It was, perhaps, the quietest dinner in some time. Even the two little boys were well-behaved, and the baby was fast asleep strapped to her mother. Bev watched each person, letting her gaze linger on Collin as she debated *good actor or thick* over and over again.

The whole room jumped when the front door swung open. Bev held her breath—was it the soldier from earlier? But as the figure sloughed off her thick cloak and the scarf dropped from her face, Bev let out a sigh.

"Etheldra," Bev said. "To what do we owe the pleasure?"

Chapter Thirteen

"It's dinner time, is it not?" Etheldra said, hanging her cloak on the hook by the front door. "Or am I no longer welcome to dine here?"

"Of course you are," Bev said, sliding off her stool to greet her properly. "I thought you'd decided to steer clear for a while."

"Well, I changed my mind based on recent events."

Bev opened and closed her mouth as Etheldra served herself, making sure to take three pieces of rosemary bread, and promptly sat at the table with Bernie, Paul, and Wallace.

"Evening, gentlemen," she said, very matter-of-factly. "I hope you don't mind me sitting here."

Something told Bev that even if the gentlemen *had* minded, Etheldra wouldn't be leaving.

"Of course not," Bernie said with a genuine smile. "We're glad to have you. I was so pleased to visit your tea shop today—"

"I'm sure." Etheldra's pointed glare made the jovial man wither a bit. Bev worried the blunt, taciturn woman would be a little *too* direct. "So, you've all been stuck in town for a few days. How are you carrying on?"

"Well, it would be better, of course, if we could move on," Paul said. "We have paid engagements that were supposed to get us through the rest of the winter. Don't even want to think about what might happen if we don't make them."

"Then leave." Etheldra stared at him so plainly the man squirmed.

Wallace jumped in to save him. "We did make an attempt today, or Paul did. But it's too crazy out there for us."

"Hm." There was doubt in her gaze, and Bev, too, wanted to speak up for Paul. But Etheldra merely turned to Bernie. "And you? Why haven't you left yet?"

"The roads, obviously," he said with a smile. "Unlike these fine gentlemen, I've already got my funds for the rest of the winter, so I don't mind staying put."

"I see." Again, that scrutinizing, untrusting glare. "And what is it you do? I saw you in my shop today reading. Seems like you have a lot of time on your hands."

"Don't we all with this weather?" he said with a chuckle. "I'm a traveling tradesman. Do a bit of everything."

"I see."

Bev opened her mouth to intervene when Etheldra turned in her chair to stare directly at Collin, who was sitting alone at the third table. "And you. What do you do?"

"Oh, I play the lute," Collin said with a smile. "I could go get it, if you—"

"I'll pay you two gold coins to never play it in my presence again," Etheldra said, pulling two coins out of her purse and tossing them over.

His mouth fell open as he greedily snatched the coins from the air. "T-thank you. I'll keep it away for tonight."

"And every night I see you, understood? If I wanted to hear an animal dying, I'd go across the street to the butchers."

He glared, but the money seemed to soothe his ego enough to keep his mouth shut.

"You seem to be a man in need of money," Etheldra said to Collin. "Do you have any other skills to speak of?"

"N-not really," he said, pocketing the coins.

"You're young and upright," she said. "Surely, you can use those hands for something other than making a racket."

"I can, but I don't want to," Collin said with a scowl as he rose. "Nor *should* I have to." He snatched his bowl off the table and brought it to Bev angrily. "Who is this lady, anyway?"

"Owner of the local tea shop," Bev said quietly, taking his bowl. "Don't take anything she says personally. She's that sort of person. But you did earn two gold coins out of it."

"True," he said. "You know, I think I might try to make a break for it tomorrow. I don't know what I'll do if I can't play my gig. I could stand to lose a toe or two, but I can't go a whole season without any money."

"You could hang around Etheldra, and she'll pay you not to play," Bev said with a chuckle.

He didn't seem to find it amusing. "I'll see you in the morning. Good night."

He left, and Bev turned her attention back to Etheldra, who seemed to have moved on to Paul and Wallace.

"So, clergyman," Etheldra said. "I don't see any religious texts with you. Are you sure that's what you do?"

Bev let out a nervous chuckle. "I don't think they wanted to risk their books being covered with dinner."

"Or ale," Etheldra said, eyeing Wallace. "You smell like you've been bathing in it. Is it common for a cleric to be so fond of drink?"

"Well, we aren't a monolith," Wallace said, forcing a smile onto his face that was probably more due to his head than Etheldra's questions.

"What's your specialty?" Etheldra asked. "I hear you all have a special interest. Do you like threatening people if they don't comply with the church's wishes?"

"Goodness me, nothing like that," Wallace said. "I pride myself in solving interpersonal disputes. Mediations, that sort of thing. Helping those who are at complete odds come to a mutually satisfying resolution."

Bev shook herself. Wallace certainly hadn't mentioned that before.

"That's a nice ring you have for a cleric," Etheldra said, nodding to his left hand. "Seems expensive. You could sell that for a nice sum and leave all the proselytizing behind."

"But would that be as fulfilling?" He looked at his husband with a smile that wasn't returned. "This ring has sentimental value to me, so I would be heartbroken if we were parted."

"Hmph." Etheldra turned to Paul. "And you—"

"I think I've had enough for one evening," Paul said, rising. "Good evening to you, Ms. Etheldra." He walked his plate over to Bev. "Whoever this woman is, I would pay double to never see her again."

"Sorry she's so blunt," Bev said, taking his plate. "Have a good night."

Paul didn't respond, but the death glare he gave his husband was enough to get the cleric to rise and bring Bev his plate and follow Paul up the stairs. Soon it was the Wersts, Bernie, and Etheldra.

Bev held her breath, hoping Etheldra would point her attention toward Bernie, but instead she stood up, dragged her chair across the room, and joined the Wersts.

"Evening," Etheldra said.

"E-evening," Abigail replied. "Boys, hurry up. It's bedtime."

"You're brave traveling across the country with such young children," she said. "You must be made of strong stuff—or have a very good reason to be headed where you're headed."

"Well, I haven't seen my parents in ages," Abigail said, a tight but friendly smile on her face. "They've never met Pascal, and he's almost three. We thought it was a good time to make the trip since I can't get away any other time of year."

"Busy at work?" Etheldra eyed her. "What do you do?"

"Oh, um. I work for the local government," Abigail said, a little nervously. "And so does Byron."

"Doing what?"

"Um… Well…"

"Spit it out, girl. We don't have all night."

"I actually work for the queen," Abigail said, her voice dropping.

Bev had to school her emotions to hide her surprise. *How did I miss that?*

"In what capacity?" Etheldra asked.

"I'm the head registrar of our city," Abigail said, her pale face bright pink now.

Bev frowned. "What in the world is that?"

Abigail laughed, as if the question were absurd. "A registrar? Surely, you've heard of them."

Bev shook her head. "Then again, if I had, perhaps it got lost with the rest of my memory."

"Well," Abigail began, looking a little less nervous, "after the war, in order to gain immunity from their wartime…actions, every kingside soldier was required to register with a local bureau. That registration needs to be updated every year to ensure they're getting the support they need from the crown."

Bev had to school her expression. She was sure a soldier like Vellora would disagree with *that* framing of the situation.

"But over time, they move, the letter gets lost in the post, that sort of thing. So investigators like Byron go looking for them to get their information updated," she said. "We've managed to organize it so he doesn't have to travel more than an hour away, usually. It's quite a good set up."

"Do others go farther?" Bev asked, thinking of Vellora.

"If the soldier has, then yes. It's based on where you registered originally," Abigail said. "Why do you ask?"

"No reason," Bev said, forcing herself to ignore the look of superiority on Etheldra's face.

"Well, I don't see a reason you should've been secretive about your job," Etheldra said. "It's just paperwork. Nothing to be ashamed of."

"I'm not ashamed, more concerned for my *very* small children," Abigail said, giving a death glare to Bev. "After all, the butcher across the street scared the daylights out of poor Estera, and she was just a foot soldier. I don't know what she'd do if she found out who I was."

"Vellora won't be coming over to bother you, I promise," Bev said with a nod. "If she did, she'd lose her business here for good. I don't tolerate that sort of thing."

"You tolerated it for Estera," Abigail said with an

uncharacteristically cold tone. "You've been over to the butcher shop every day since she left like there's nothing amiss. You're hosting their solstice party. Her wife was here decorating the tree."

"And as I recall, you were pleased your boys could participate," Bev said with a look. "I promise, the butchers mean you no harm, and Vellora got a good talking to. She's not a danger to anyone, unless they're a danger to her family."

"Estera? A danger?" Abigail scoffed. "That's the most ridiculous thing... The girl was barely old enough to carry a sword, let alone be a *danger* to anyone."

Bev sensed an opportunity. "I think the concern was about the party she was traveling with—the soldiers."

"As long as the butchers aren't doing anything illegal, there's nothing for them to worry about," Abigail said, rising with a dark look. "Come, boys, it's time for bed. Hopefully, the snow will melt, and we can get out of this town tomorrow."

"But I'm not—" Byron began, his mouth still full of food.

"*Now*, Byron."

The family trotted up the stairs, Bev watching them with a frown. "You can't intimidate my guests like this, Etheldra."

"Nothing I said was intimidating," she replied,

turning her attention to Bernie. "Unless there was something *to* intimidate."

"You didn't see that butcher threaten that poor young soldier," Bernie replied. "Just ghastly the way she nearly throttled that young girl."

"As I said," Etheldra eyed Bernie, "when one believes their family is threatened, they'll do whatever it takes to protect them."

Bernie met her gaze with an easygoing smile. "To my eyes, it seems everyone overreacted. I hear you've had some trouble with queen's soldiers in the past few months. That certainly puts people on edge. And Estera keeping her job and nearby regiment quiet..." He shrugged. "I could see why the butcher thought there was something nefarious afoot." It was his turn to rise with his empty plate. "I suppose it's all well now, considering Estera's been gone for days and that soldier returned to his regiment today. But one might want to warn the butcher to keep her temper in case they make a reappearance." He nodded toward the stairs. "And that there's an official registrar in town, too."

"Vellora's got a lot to be upset about, but she's not going to threaten a mother and children. She does have a heart, you know." Etheldra crossed her arms and watched him. "Good evening to you."

"And to you, Ms. Etheldra."

Even though the front room was empty, Etheldra insisted Bev join her in the privacy of the kitchen, going as far as to walk over to the crackling fire to instruct Biscuit to stand by the door to check for eavesdroppers.

"He won't—" Bev began, but the laelaps trotted to the door and sat down. "Well, I guess he will."

"To the matter at hand," Etheldra said, snapping her fingers. "The cleric and his husband, bard, and traveler are all in need of money. And the parents, well, being affiliated with the queen might be enough."

"Traveler... Bernie? He has plenty of money," Bev said.

"He seems the kind of man who wants to get it as easily as he can," Etheldra said. "Nasty sort, don't like to work hard."

"You got all that from a five-minute conversation with him?"

"Of course I did. I see people for who they are."

"Well, you said everyone has a motive—what motive do Abigail and Byron have? They don't need money, obviously. She indicated they were well-off with her job."

"Perhaps it's not about money—"

"The letters are pretty clear that it is," Bev replied. "But what *exactly* is the point of the registrar? I doubt they're...what was it? Providing services."

"Of course not," Etheldra said. "Some are better than others, of course. I'm sure that young mother believes she's doing the soldiers a kindness. But it's probably not very comforting for someone to send you a letter listing every battle you fought in and asking you to re-sign your loyalty to the queen you waged war against. And if you *don't* respond to that letter, they show up at your front door, making sure you aren't involved in any treasonous activities." She tilted her head. "Or married to any magic-wielding women."

"Abigail is from the west," Bev said. "Vellora, as far as I know, is from the south."

Etheldra shrugged. "You might ask Vellora when's the last time she got in touch with *her* registrar. Maybe there's something amiss there."

"I still say that with the magic hunters nearby, it makes the most sense that Ida would be the target, not Vellora."

Etheldra didn't look convinced. "I hope my questions were enlightening. I certainly got a lot from them."

Bev resisted the urge to argue, as every one of her guests had left in a huff, except Bernie, who seemed impervious to Etheldra's bluntest questions. "So who do you think is behind the letters?"

"I don't know, Bev. That's your job to figure

out."

She shook her head weakly. "No, actually, it's—"

"But if I were you, I'd get more from that family. Not to say the parents are sending the letters —if they were, I'd be impressed they have that much time on their hands. But it's possible they said something to one of the other guests."

"So far, the bard's the only one I can plausibly suspect," Bev said. "He knew Estera belonged to the magic hunters before anyone else, and the timeline works out that—"

Etheldra barked a laugh. "That idiot? He can't find his way out of a paper bag."

"Or he's a good liar."

She shook her head. "You know I've got a feeling for these things. The only thing the bard is hiding is his own idiocy—and he can't even do that well. Talk to the family tomorrow and see what you uncover." She turned to walk to the door. "Vellora might insist she's done all the right things, but the queen's people have a way of making the right thing wrong—especially out here. So as much as you think it's Ida, don't discount the possibility that Vellora's the target, or you might miss the real culprit."

Chapter Fourteen

Bev had lain awake all night, staring at the ceiling with Biscuit softly snoring between her heels. She'd been so focused on Ida's magic that while she'd certainly *considered* the idea that Vellora might be the target, she hadn't taken it very seriously. And Etheldra was right—the queen's people had proven time and again that they could bend the rules when they wanted to.

More questions, few answers.

More snow had fallen overnight, but the sky was clear as Bev donned her thick coat to check on Sin and the Wersts' horse in the stable. It had been several days since she'd made it out to Herman's house, and the goats were probably in need of refreshing. She wasn't looking forward to the long trek, but it would get her out of the inn, and perhaps some of her guests would do as they'd threatened and leave—especially since it felt a few degrees warmer.

Bev finished the rest of her chores and, although she didn't want to, sat to wait for her guests to come down. The Mysterious H was first, of course, storming down the stairs dressed in his full cloak and head wrap. Bev hadn't even *mentioned* him to Etheldra, but she had enough on her plate as it was.

"You're welcome to try," Bev said as he opened the door.

He turned, said nothing, and headed toward the front door, leaving without a word.

Surprisingly, the next person down the stairs was Wallace, looking quite rough around the edges as he sought food and water. Bev was able to provide the latter, which he took with gratitude.

"Allen should be here shortly with the breakfast goodies," Bev said. "It'll probably be biscuits again, but—"

"Oh, those are fine," Wallace croaked, sucking down the water Bev had handed him. "Just a bit tired this morning, you know. Couldn't get comfortable."

Tired. Hungover was more like it. "I'm sorry to

hear that," Bev said.

"And I must offer my sincere apologies for taking advantage of your hospitality," Wallace said, managing to turn on that godly tone even through his obvious exhaustion. "My husband tells me I've been too zealous with the ale, and that I've nearly cleared you out."

"Yes, I mentioned that to you yesterday afternoon," Bev said. How drunk had the cleric *really* been? "Don't you remember?"

"Ah, well, yesterday was something of a..." He cleared his throat as he twisted his ring. "In any case, I promise I'll steer clear for the duration of our stay. Which I hope will end today..." He smiled, though it was clear his head was hurting. "Is that possible, do you think?"

"As I told Collin last night, everyone is welcome to try their luck on the roads," Bev said. "But we had another inch fall overnight, so if you're looking for an improvement, you aren't going to get it."

He sighed. "My husband will be so disappointed. We may not be making it to Kaiser Tuckey's house after all. He was so looking forward to the payday."

"He seems to be the one holding your pursestrings," Bev said. "And I mean that in the most complimentary way."

Wallace laughed. "He's miserly, that's for sure.

But if it wasn't for him, I'd probably sit around all day waxing poetic about the nature of religion and drinking too much wine. He's the one who arranges my visits, collects and manages the money, that sort of thing. I'd be hopelessly lost trying to figure all that out." He paused, cracking a wry smile. "And if it wasn't for me, he'd be back in Luwood village, counting coins for some rich person and trying to squeeze them for every silver he could."

Would that extend to the butchers, too? "How long have you been together?"

"Thirty years almost," he said with a sigh. "Seems like yesterday we tied the knot under a flower-filled tree near the river."

"That's a long time, for sure," Bev said. "You must be very proud of your marriage." She paused, finding a natural segue. "The last wedding I attended was that of the butchers across the street about two years ago. You met Ida the other day."

"And her wife, briefly," Wallace said with a nod. "They seem like a lovely, well-matched couple. Fate will certainly smile on them for a long time." He paused, turning to look at the solstice tree. "Especially with as much care as Ida puts into decorating her tree. It's certainly magnificent. And amazing that she was able to bring it all by herself." He turned to Bev. "Is she…special?"

"Special?" Bev asked, her suspicions raised

immediately. "In what way?"

"Touched by magic?" he asked.

"If she is, she doesn't know it," Bev said. "That's who Ida is. But you know, looks can be deceiving. The tree is large, but it's not incredibly heavy."

"Oh, I've carried my share of solstice trees, and they're both sometimes!" He chuckled. "Fear not, I'm not going to damn her for carrying the magic in her veins. But I do find it interesting to see the different ways it manifests. Is she descended from gnomes? Dwarfs?"

Bev cleared her throat, not liking where this conversation was going. "As I said, if she's got magic in her veins, it's news to her and the rest of us. Where or how she got it—"

"But surely, that's why you were talking with the librarian about her family tree?" Wallace said. To Bev's quizzical stare, he added, "Paul mentioned that he overheard you two talking about her family tree."

"She was interested in some ancient history with her distant cousins in Middleburg," Bev said. "I was trying to help out since I was there. It's mostly about who should've inherited her butcher shop a hundred years ago."

"Well, that's a shame," he said with a shake of his head. "I think everyone should dig as deeply into their magical history as they like."

"The queen seems to have a problem with that line of thinking," Bev said.

"Oh, her? She's in Queen's Capital. What influence does she have all the way out here?"

Bev watched him, unable to sense if his devil-may-care attitude was real or an act.

Their conversation came to an abrupt stop when Allen walked through the front door with a basket of his breakfast biscuits, dried meat, and cheese. Wallace helped himself as Allen put the basket on the table. The baker then made a move like he wanted to speak with Bev in private, so she followed him into the kitchen, closing the door behind her.

"So you asked me to keep an eye on that mysterious, grumpy stranger?" Allen said. "Well, I still don't know his name, but I can tell you that he comes in early every morning, gets a pastry, then heads north."

Bev's eyes widened. "Are you sure?"

He nodded. "Still don't have his name, but I thought you should know. Especially since I hear there are soldiers up that way."

"Bev?" Wallace walked into the kitchen. "Oh, here you both are. I wanted to extend my compliments to the excellent baker. You've certainly kept us well-fed in the morning, especially with these, what do we call them?"

"Breakfast biscuits," Bev said with a smile as she

gestured for the group to leave the kitchen, heading back to the front room.

Wallace didn't let Allen leave for at least an hour, peppering him with questions about baking and where the recipe for the biscuits came from. Allen was cordial, answering as best he could, and none of the questions veered into the magical as they'd done with Bev. In fact, Wallace seemed more concerned that there wasn't a local clergyman in town.

"Surely, the townsfolk need some spiritual guidance," he said to Bev after Allen had excused himself to return to the bakery. "There must be someone nearby who can preside over the rituals. Or at least weddings, funerals?"

"There's someone in Middleburg who makes the trip, if needed," Bev said. "But no, I think we're far too small a village to have that sort of need."

"You have a library," Wallace said with a frown.

"More of an archive," Bev replied. "Fascinating if you'd like to know how many pounds of potatoes were harvested in a given year. But the book selection is quite limited—as your husband found out, I'm sure. I—"

The front door opened, and the Mysterious H came back inside, knocking his boots on the mat. He crossed the room, placed one silver on the counter then headed upstairs.

"Chatty fellow, isn't he?" Wallace said with a laugh as he twisted the red ring around his pinky. "Seems eager to leave."

"So he says," Bev said. "But he ends up back here after about half an hour. One would think he'd get tired of trying…"

Unless he wasn't trying to leave at all.

Bev was convinced *he* was the "mysterious stranger" coming and going from Allen's bakery early in the morning. But did that make him the blackmailer? And if so, how was Bev going to find proof?

Further conversation was diverted when Bernie appeared, and Bev put her suspicions about the Mysterious H in her back pocket. "Breakfast biscuits on the menu this morning, Bernie."

The traveler frowned. "Nothing sweet for us today?"

"I believe Allen is saving the sweets for Etheldra's tea shop," Bev said. "She pays him a bit better than I do."

"You know, I'm quite fond of these," Wallace said, helping himself to a second. "They're hearty and filling with the meat and cheese. Gives you good energy for seizing the day. Even if it's sitting around waiting for the snow to melt."

"Oh, tell me it's melted." Abigail descended the stairs with the rest of her family in tow. They all looked ready to travel, and it pained Bev to have to tell them otherwise.

"We had more snow fall overnight," she said. "I can help get your wagon put together, if you'd like to try."

"Yes, that would be lovely," Abigail said with a nervous look. "Thank you."

Bev helped Byron clear off the wagon and pack the Wersts' large steamer trunk on top while Abigail and the children ate breakfast and kept warm by the fire.

"I wanted to apologize about last night," Bev said. "Etheldra's a blunt sort of woman, and if you aren't used to her, she can be a lot. But she does mean well, and I promise you that the butchers across the street mean you no harm."

"I think we're all going a bit stir-crazy," Byron said with a nod. "Abby's nervous we won't make it to her parents in time for Margo's first solstice, and the boys were so looking forward to the festivities. Not to mention, we've only got so many days until we need to get back to work."

Work. Probably best not to ask about it quite yet. "Well, I hated the thought of you leaving with a bad taste about Pigsend in your mouth."

He smiled. "Not to worry. We've been so grateful for your hospitality and patience."

The horse was hooked to the front of the wagon as Abigail and the children came out. She frowned at the snow, the wagon, and the state of things, but climbed up anyway. "Well, we'll see how far we get."

"You're going west, right?" Bev asked, and they nodded. "Look, I've got to get out to Herman Monday's farm to check on his goats. Why don't I walk with you along the road and help the horse and wagon?"

Abigail opened her mouth to argue, but Byron shook his head. "I think we could use all the help we can get."

They'd barely made it out of the backyard before even Abigail started to look like she regretted their decision. The sun shone bright overhead and there was a shimmery layer atop the snow as it melted, but the sheer amount that had fallen made it almost impossible for the horse to walk and the wagon wheels to turn.

"Abby," Byron said, turning to his wife as Bev pulled their horse forward. "We really should reconsider. If this weather holds up, we might have an easier go of it tomorrow."

"I have to agree," Bev huffed as the horse protested. "I think we might finally have that break in the weather we've been looking for. But I don't think you're even going to make it to Middleburg in this—"

The horse neighed and bucked, sending Bev backward. She scrambled forward, but it was too late—they must've gone too far off the hidden road, as the wagon and all its occupants landed in a ditch.

"Margo, sweet baby," Abigail gasped, looking down at the baby strapped to her front. The child was red-faced and screaming but seemed otherwise okay. "Boys? Are you all right?"

"Fine, Mama," they chimed as their father and Bev pulled them out of the snow and upright.

"Oh, no…" Byron said, turning to look at their wagon. It was on its side, buried in the snowbank, the wheels spinning haphazardly. The horse had broken its bonds and managed to escape, but it looked annoyed to even be out there.

"Our wagon…" Abigail whispered, putting her hand to her forehead as she bounced the baby. "Byron… What are we going to do? We never should've left."

"Let me see about getting some help," Bev said. She opened her mouth to recommend Ida, but… wasn't it a risk to show off her great strength in front of these two queen's servants?

Luckily, the answer came in the form of a shouting figure in a house nearby. Ramone was recognizable from their dramatic purple cloak swung around their shoulders. They hurried through the snow, perhaps having heard the commotion.

"Ramone." Bev waved. "Can you give us a hand?"

The sculptor approached, their hand coming to their mouth. "What in the world happened?"

"The family wanted to get on the road," Bev said, a little helplessly. There was an *I-told-you-so* on the tip of her tongue, but she honestly felt horrible for Abigail and Byron.

"You poor dears," Ramone said. "Oh, with the little ones, too? What in the world were you thinking, taking a horse and wagon out in these conditions?"

Abigail sniffed, tears coming down as little Peter joined his siblings in holding onto his mother and crying. "I wanted to get somewhere safe."

"There's no safer place than the Weary Dragon in Pigsend," Ramone said softly, walking over. They put their hand on Peter's head and the young boy looked up in wonder. "There, now. You had a bit of a scare, but you're all unscathed, aren't you?"

The little boy nodded.

"What are we going to do about the wagon?" Byron asked. "Do you think the three of us can pull it out?"

"It's good and stuck for the moment," Ramone said, inspecting it. "We'll need to get Ida to pull this wagon out of the ditch."

"Ida? Who's Ida?" Byron asked.

"She's the—"

"I have a better idea," Bev said, stopping Ramone before they spilled the beans. "Why don't we leave the wagon and take the children and horse back to the inn. Ramone can keep an eye on it, but I'm sure no one will bother it."

"No one is even *out*, except you fool...er, *fine* people," Ramone said. "Look, the poor children are freezing. Bring the horse to my stable and come in for a hot cup of tea to warm up. Tomorrow, we'll see about getting your wagon unstuck and you on your way."

CHAPTER FIFTEEN

Even with the warm sun, the snow was cold and wet, so all were pleased to take off cloaks and boots and sit by Ramone's fire. Even Bev, who considered herself a hearty sort of woman, was happy to be out of the snow. Ramone told them to make themselves at home while the sculptor tended to the horse, putting him in the empty barn and finding some hay and water.

"You're welcome to leave him here, too," they said upon their return. "Beautiful creature. But quite annoyed you brought him out in this."

Abigail wiped her red-rimmed eyes. "I know. I shouldn't have. But I just... I'm sorry. I was so fearful of staying."

"You don't have to apologize," Bev said. "I understand. But I promise the butchers mean you no harm. They're rather lovely people, once you get to know them."

"The loveliest." Ramone nodded as they walked back inside. "Now, Bev, come help me get them some tea."

Bev helped Ramone bring in a set of beautifully painted teacups, and immediately, Abigail shook her head violently. "Oh, the boys will destroy them!"

"And I'll be happy to be rid of them," Ramone said with a scoff, handing one to the younger boy. "My dastardly brother painted them."

"I didn't realize you had a brother, Ramone," Bev said. "Is he local?"

Ramone's face darkened, and Bev got the distinct impression that the topic was about as contentious as Kaiser Tuckey.

"Be *careful*," Abigail said to her boys, hovering over them nervously. "Still, they shouldn't make a mess. We've already broken enough of your things."

"Oh?" Ramone sat. "Oh! Right. Bev mentioned that one of the vases had broken." They gestured to the room. "You're welcome to take your pick of anything in the room, Bev. It all needs to go."

"Does it?" Bev asked. "Why?"

"Well." They smiled, their eyes lighting up in a

way Bev hadn't seen before. "I think I'm finally past whatever dark cloud has been over my head these past few months. I've got a *brilliant* design for the new Pigsend fountain." They began describing a creature Bev couldn't even start to understand, but she got the distinct impression it was going to be massive, ornate, and brilliant. "Yes, it feels like a new day has dawned, and all is right with the world."

"Oh, Ramone, that's absolutely wonderful." Bev pressed her hand to her heart. "I'm sure it'll be magnificent."

"So, as you can see, I need to clear everything out of this place so I have room to work. And since you have such wonderful helpers," they beamed at the boys, "take as much as you want. I'm sure there's more than a few cast-off dragon figurines around here, too. Take them all. I don't want *anything* getting in the way of my creative flow."

"If you're sure," Abigail said, looking around. "Boys—"

But they were faster, diving off the couch to select their playthings and making roaring sounds as they fought each other on the table.

"Seems like this ended well after all," Byron said with a look at Abigail and Bev.

"And when the snow melts, we'll see about getting your wagon out of that ditch and back on the road." Ramone took Abigail's hand and squeezed it. "But in the meantime, don't feel unsafe at the Weary Dragon. Bev is the kindest, most genuine person, and the butchers...well, Vellora's a bit of a hothead, but only when it comes to protecting that wife of hers. One can understand making ridiculous decisions to keep one's family safe, hm?"

Abigail's cheeks reddened a bit as she squeezed Ramone's hand. "I suppose you're right."

"Of course I am."

⁓

Ramone insisted the boys take ten figurines each (and that was negotiated down from a whole box of them) and made Bev and Byron take two vases under each arm. Then they walked the family and Bev to the front of their property.

"This is where we part," they said with a kind smile. "I hope to see you tomorrow."

"Us too," Abigail said.

"Ramone, if you're willing to make the walk, I'd love to have you at the inn this evening for dinner," Bev said. "As a thank you for all your hospitality."

"Hm... Will you be making your rosemary bread?"

"Of course," Bev said with a nod. "Every night."

"Then I'm there."

With the two little boys leading the way, the group made their way back to the Weary Dragon.

Even though their wagon was in a ditch, Abigail and Byron seemed a bit less harried than before, and for that, Bev was happy.

"I honestly don't know much about Ramone, other than they used to be a sculptor for Kaiser Tuckey," Bev said. "But they've always been a kind soul. I'm glad they were able to put you at ease."

"Well, perhaps I did overreact a little," Abigail said, huffing and puffing as she kept her hand over the baby's head. "I can't believe I thought *this* was okay to leave in. Good thing our kids didn't freeze to death."

"You seem to handle that baby pretty well," Bev said. "Must be exhausting having her strapped to you all day."

"I carried her for nine months, what's a few more?" Abigail said with a chuckle. "She actually comes with me to work. I did the same for the boys, too."

"That's even more impressive," Bev said with a small whistle. "You both working with three littles. Must be chaotic."

"We're able to make our own schedule, so we end up taking turns a lot," Abigail said. "And Byron's family is nearby. I'm the one who decided to move cross-country from her family." She snorted. "But I couldn't say no to the career opportunity."

"It's wonderful that your employers are so family-friendly."

"Her Majesty has made family values a priority, and insists upon flexibility," Abigail said. "It's one of the reasons I'm so happy to work for her. Everyone at my office is so patient with the children. And across our travels, too, we've encountered such lovely people. The clerics have been quite patient with the boys, and sweet Collin, too." Her face darkened. "The only one who's given us problems is that curmudgeon who never shows his face."

"Don't tell me he's been bothering you still," Bev said with a frown. "Because that's not acceptable."

"He hasn't said anything, no, but he's been rather loud about the boys from his room. Banging on the wall, that sort of thing. I can't blame him for being tired of it. They're my own kids, and they wear me out almost every day."

Bev had to smile as the boys tumbled over a large snowbank as they chased one another. "They're children. That's what they do, I hear."

They walked the rest of the way in comfortable silence, watching the boys and Byron ahead as the Weary Dragon came into view. But although Bev hadn't ever suspected the Wersts as possible blackmailers, she still rather wished they'd given her something to move the investigation forward, as

Etheldra had said they would. But Bev didn't have the heart to pry, not when Abigail finally seemed to trust her again.

As the group hurried into the inn, knocking slushy snow from their boots and wiping their muddy feet, they were greeted by Bernie and Wallace, who didn't seem surprised to see the family return. Bev and Byron placed the vases on the tables, far out of reach of the boys, who scampered upstairs to continue playing with their dragon figurines.

"It's a mess out there," Bernie said. "But the sun is shining, so that's a blessing."

"Truly," Wallace agreed. "And we're grateful you made it back in one piece."

"Thanks to Bev and the wonderful citizens of Pigsend," Abigail said. "Ramone Comely was their name?"

Bev nodded.

"Oh, that sounds familiar," Wallace said, putting his hand to his chin. "Why does that name sound familiar?"

"They used to work for Kaiser Tuckey," Bev said. "Perhaps you've met them in the past?"

"Yes!" Wallace brightened. "Yes, now I remember. Oh, wait, no." He shook his head. "No, it wasn't Ramone Comely, it was someone else named Comely working as the artist there. Does

Ramone have a sibling?"

"As a matter of fact, they do," Bev said. "And that probably explains why they got so grumpy when I mentioned both."

"Siblings, what are you going to do?" Wallace chuckled, turning the red ring on his finger. "Still, this Ramone has quite the talent. These vases are beautiful."

Bev wasn't an expert in art, but she had to agree. "You can tell them yourself when they come to dinner tonight."

"Will Etheldra be making another appearance?" Bernie asked.

"I can't be sure, but I doubt it," Bev said. It seemed the old woman had asked the questions she'd wanted, and decided her job was finished. "So it'll be us and Ramone this evening. Just…uh… nobody mention Kaiser or Ramone's sibling. Tends to make things a bit dicey."

"Noted," Wallace said with a chuckle. "I can't imagine Mr. Tuckey firing such an incredible artist, though."

"I'm not sure of the whole story," she said. "And as I said, it seems to be a sensitive subject, so I'm not about to ask." She glanced at the clock. How had it gotten so late? "If you fine gentlemen want to locate a spot for these new art pieces, I'd appreciate it. I've got to get into the kitchen."

Ida had already delivered her meat order, so Bev prepared quickly as Biscuit followed her around, eager for a scrap to tide him over until he was inevitably fed by Peter and Pascal.

Dinner was served at six, and although everyone had been stuck at the inn for nearly a week now, there was a sense that things were improving. The sun had been shining all day, and even as it set, the cold wind that had been howling was absent.

"Perhaps God is smiling on us," Wallace said. "He wouldn't ruin the solstice for us."

"Hopefully not," Paul said with a look.

The Werst family, still exhausted from their ordeal earlier in the day, ate little and headed upstairs, leaving Wallace, Paul, Bernie, and Collin sitting around a single table, eating quietly. Bev glanced at the clock—it was getting close to seven now.

"Wasn't that artist coming?" Wallace asked.

"Supposedly," Bev said with a frown. "But maybe they got waylaid."

Just as she spoke, the front door opened, and Ramone swept into the room, looking dramatic in a red cloak and fancy hat that probably did little to dispel the cold. Bev introduced them to the rest of the group, and they shook every hand before coming to stand in front of Bev with a pleased look.

"You know, every so often the wind blows the

right way, and I get a whiff of whatever you're cooking here," Ramone said. "I'm pleased I finally get to partake."

"You're welcome here any night," Bev said, handing them a plate. "Now fill up and sit wherever you'd like."

"Oh, please come join our table," Bernie said, patting the open seat beside him.

Wallace nodded emphatically, though his husband didn't share his enthusiasm. "I'd love to hear more about how you produce your art. You are most talented."

Ramone beamed as they served themselves and made their way over to their admirers' table. "I should've had more dinners here. You're too kind."

"I mean, I've seen some art in the cities," Bernie said. "And yours is absolutely on par with it. What would you say you'd sell it for?"

"Oh, I'm long past selling my castoffs for profit," they said. "These are silly little trifles, meant to pass the time."

"I hardly believe that," Wallace said, pointing to the vase in the center of the table. "I mean, look at the detail, the artistry!"

Bev smiled as Ramone blushed, hiding their face and giggling. "You two are trying to puff me up, aren't you?"

Their conversation came to an abrupt end as a

door upstairs opened and closed loudly, and the only person not in the dining room came storming down the stairs, still wrapped in his cloak, scarf hiding his face. Bev perked up, forcing a smile onto her face as Mysterious H approached and slapped a silver down on the counter.

"Good to see you again," Bev said. "Will you be joining us for dinner?"

"Well, since the *price* of service has gone up," he snapped, turning to give a death glare to Collin. But his dark eyes landed on Ramone, and his entire body stiffened. "I have to go."

Ramone rose, almost in disbelief. "It can't be..."

"What's wrong?" Bev asked. "Where are you—"

"Must be off." H raced toward the door, but Ramone let out a loud gasp and pointed at him.

"*Stop him!*"

Bernie and Byron were closest, grabbing H by the arms as he passed and keeping him from running out the door. Bev didn't know *what* the man was thinking, especially since there was nowhere for him to go beyond the inn.

Ramone walked up to H with a scowl on their face. "You have a lot of nerve showing up here, you cretin."

H lifted his chin, his face still hidden. Bev was shocked Ramone could recognize him. "I wasn't *planning* on staying here, you oaf. But the snow disrupted my plans."

"Leaving or coming from your *evil* employer?" Ramone asked. "I hear he's got great solstice plans this year."

"You mean Kaiser?" Bev asked, but Ramone shushed her.

"I don't have to answer to you. It's not my fault you were fired."

That certainly answered that. "Ramone, I don't think you should accost this poor man for taking the job you were fired from," Bev began.

"It's more than this oaf taking my job. He was also our parents' favorite!"

Bev shook herself. "W-what? This is your brother?"

H removed his scarf to reveal a face not dissimilar to Ramone's, complete with the matching scowl. "Yes, if you *must* be so nosy. My name is Horst Comely, and this ignoramus is my sibling."

CHAPTER SIXTEEN

"S-siblings!" Bev gasped. Of all the inns in the country... And based on the animosity between them, there seemed to be a good reason Horst had wanted his identity to remain a secret.

"We were certainly *raised* together, but this no-good lout lost the chance to call himself my sibling when he betrayed me." Ramone huffed, lifting their nose into the air.

"I didn't betray anyone, you two-bit amateur," Horst shot back. "You lost the job thanks to your whimsical nature. Kaiser said—"

"Oh, that name!" Ramone turned and put their hand on their head dramatically. "I can't hear that name!"

"*He* said you hadn't sculpted anything in months when he let you go," Horst said. "He gave you several generous warnings to stop messing around and create something. He's not in the business of giving money for nothing."

"I can't help it that the muse does what it wants," they said, waving to the air with a flourish. "No wonder I've been so creatively stuck for weeks. What with you stinking up the halls of my former patron's home."

"I haven't *been* there for weeks," Horst said. "In fact, I was *returning* there when all this confounded snow fell. I'm sure he's going to be furious with me for delaying my arrival."

"Surely, he'll have some sympathy for you," Wallace said, coming to stand next to the siblings. "We're headed to his house as well, and we've been unable to leave."

"We?" Horst narrowed his gaze. "Who is we?"

"Myself, my husband, and dear Collin the bard," Wallace said. "I'm supposed to lead the solstice service, and Collin will be playing the music. But alas, we're stuck here, same as you." He brightened. "Oh, how fortuitous that we're all going to the same place."

Ramone let out a scoff of disgust. "You *would* take his side."

"Now, Ramone," Bev said, "there's no need to be rude. You and Horst clearly have some bad blood, but—"

"It's more than bad blood," Ramone said.

"It's them being ridiculous," Horst replied.

"Let me have a go," Wallace said, holding his hand up to Bev. "Why don't we all sit down over a pint and discuss this?"

"Ahem." Paul shook his head.

"You can have pints, I'll…well, I suppose I'll listen," Wallace replied with a nervous smile.

Bev hadn't expected them to agree to it, but the siblings sat on opposite sides of the table, crossing their arms over their chests in an almost identical manner.

"Now, why don't we start at the beginning?" Wallace said. "Ramone, why don't you go first?"

"Simple. I was the chosen sculptor for Kaiser Tuckey up until two years ago. I'd been a faithful servant to him for ten years. Then my dastardly brother showed up and *happened* to bring a canvas. Left it lying around so Kaiser would see it. The next thing I know, *Horst* has my job, my house, my livelihood, and I'm expelled to this nothing little village with scraps of commissions to live on."

Bev frowned. She hadn't had a clue that Ramone was in dire need of money.

"That's not what happened at all," Horst said to

Wallace. "My *sibling* invited me to stay, said they were having trouble with their art. They felt stilted and jammed up, like something was blocking their creativity. So I came with some *samples* to help inspire them. Mr. Tuckey happened to see one, and he liked my style."

"And fired me!"

"You were already on the brink of being fired," Horst replied. "You hadn't made a piece of art in six months. *Hence* why you contacted me to come help."

"And were you two…?" Wallace considered his words. "Are you more creative together?"

"Yes," Horst said as Ramone said, "*No.*"

"Well, that's clear as mud," Bev muttered.

"When we were children, we'd often work together on projects," Horst said. "I can't sculpt to save my life, and Ramone's skill with paint leaves a lot to be desired." He gestured to the vase on the table. "Look at this. Uneven lines, no clear vision. But the detail on the sculpted pieces is exquisite."

Bev didn't know enough about art to really say whether he was telling the truth, but Ramone seemed to take offense.

"If my skill is so bad, how did I get hired in the first place?" Ramone snorted.

"That's not what I said."

"That's exactly what you said!"

"All right, all right," Wallace said with his hands up. "So we've aired the reason for the grievance. How are we planning on resolving it?"

Nobody said anything.

"I don't want to fight with you, Ramone," Horst said. "I actually… Well, I miss you, dear sibling. And if I'm being honest, I think there's something amiss with that manor. I haven't felt creatively full since setting foot there. In fact, I've been more productive in the past few days, sitting in my room staring out the window, than in the past two years."

Ramone shifted, but Bev cleared her throat. "Didn't you also admit that you'd finally figured out what you were going to sculpt for the town fountain, Ramone?"

"Perhaps," they muttered through tight lips.

"Then perhaps being in proximity of each other is what you need," Wallace said, toying with his ring. "You know, I've heard about this sort of thing with siblings. A need for them to be near each other. Almost like magic."

The two artists stared at the clergyman with dubious expressions. "We don't have magic," Ramone replied.

"Don't you?" Wallace said, twisting the ring back and forth so quickly it was almost distracting to Bev. "There's magic in art. You create something from nothing. And it stands to reason that if you and Horst were so close in your youth, being in each other's presence is necessary to reach your full potential."

Bev quirked a brow. *That* was certainly a stretch. She didn't believe for a second that either Comely sibling was—

"Oh, *Horst*!" Ramone rose, their face covered in tears. "How could I have been so blind?"

Horst was crying as well as he raced around the table. "My dear sibling!"

"Really?" Bev said, perhaps a little too loudly. "That worked?"

Wallace chuckled and walked to Bev to give the siblings time to cry in peace. "You seem surprised, Bev. I am clergy, after all. It's my job to help mend fences."

Bev felt a little tickle in her mind, and glanced down at that infernal ring that had been distracting her. No, not distracting...tugging at her mind. "Wallace, what's in that ring of yours?"

His brows rose, surprised. "You... You can feel it?"

Bev nodded. "There's something in there, isn't it?"

"Not many people can tell, I'm impressed." He chuckled. "It's just a *bit* of magic. Helps me get to the bottom of what's really bothering people without the effort of having to draw it out of them." He glanced over his shoulder. "For these two, they wanted to know they needed each other equally. Horst was on the road to forgiveness, and Ramone needed a little tug." He beamed. "All in the spirit of reconciliation."

"Is that sort of magic…legal?" Bev asked.

He gave her a nervous smile. "Perhaps not *strictly*, but I figure it's being used in the service of good, so it can't be held against me. Though I haven't exactly flaunted it in front of a queen's soldier to test that theory." He tilted his head.

Bev nodded slowly. That certainly put a new spin on the blackmail angle. Wallace couldn't possibly be so brazen as to blackmail the butchers while using illegal magic of his own, could he?

Almost on cue, Wallace cleared his throat, perhaps realizing he shouldn't have been so loose with the truth. "And if there are…"

"I'm not in the business of sharing secrets," Bev said. "Yours are safe with me."

The siblings broke apart, but not too far, with Ramone announcing, "I insist you leave this place and stay at my house. We must continue our great healing."

"Agreed, dear sibling," Horst replied with the same breathy tone. "But I'll need help. I've made lots of art in my time here."

"You...have?" Bev frowned. "What kind of art?"

"Oh...my..."

Horst clearly had left the inn much more than Bev had seen, because almost every inch of his room was covered in sketches, drawings, and paintings, all portraying a snowy Pigsend, of the people coming and going, Etheldra's tea shop, the bakery—Bev stopped counting after a while. Clearly, the banging Abigail had mentioned was the artist hanging up his work. Bev didn't exactly appreciate the new holes in her wall, but decided to leave it alone.

"Impressive." Bernie walked to the first painting.

"Where did you get all this paper?" Bev asked. "And paint? I haven't seen you leave the inn at all."

"I brought it with me," he said, carefully pulling the nails off the wall. "I'd been on sabbatical in a last-ditch effort to find inspiration so I didn't lose my job with Mr. Tuckey. But as I said, this is the first time I've felt inspired." He smiled at Ramone. "I must've known you were right down the road."

"Dear sibling, we will never be parted again," Ramone said with a sigh.

"Quite the turn," Bev muttered, pulling another nail off the wall and gently placing the landscape of a snowed-in Pigsend village on top of the rest as Wallace came up beside her to admire the work, too. "Are you sure that ring didn't have any *persuasive* abilities, either?"

Wallace chuckled, eyeing a portrait of himself and Paul reading by the fire. "I fear I've said too much about its abilities as it is."

So, yes. Bev glanced at the artists, hoping that once the spell wore off, they wouldn't go back to hating one another.

"Usually, the push is enough to heal things," Wallace said, under his breath. "And they rarely go back to their tiffs. Now, will they fight over something else? Probably." He chuckled. "That's the nature of these things, unfortunately. But for the moment, there's peace. And that's good enough for me."

He walked the portrait over to Horst, asking if he could keep it. "I've never seen my husband looking so handsome."

"Of course, of course. They're just ditties," Horst said with a smile that seemed odd after all the short-clipped gruffness. "I'm sure I'll have more to paint soon."

"Wow, I didn't think anyone liked my playing," Collin said, holding a painting of him laughing and playing the lute. "I didn't even think you'd seen me playing?"

"I peeked down that first night," Horst said. "You are quite talented, Collin. Don't let anyone tell you differently, especially that angry old woman."

"Angry old…?" Ramone turned to Bev.

"Etheldra Daws," Bev said.

"Ah, yes, ignore her. She wouldn't know good art if it bit her in the face," Ramone said with a sniff. "Brother, this? This is the best thing I've ever seen you do." He held up a painting of Vellora and Estera arguing in the backyard. "Look at the emotion, the drama. You've captured the butcher's temper perfectly."

Bev didn't think Vellora would appreciate the interpretation of her angry face, so she kept looking around the room. She found a painting of Allen and Vicky at the shop holding hands and another of Mayor Hendry walking down a snowy road.

"When did you get out and see all this?" Bev asked.

"I waited until the front room was cleared," Horst said. "Took a walk around the town once a day to get inspired and clear my head." He nodded to the painting of Vellora and Ida. "The butchers, in particular, drew my focus. They have such energy about them right now."

Bev inspected the painting again, ready to compliment him on the way he painted Vellora when she spotted a shadowy figure leaving their backyard.

"What's this?" Bev asked, pointing to the figure. "And when did you paint this?"

"On the first day. I was watching the butcher shop and saw them talking," Horst said.

"And this shadow?" Bev asked, pointing to the figure. "Did you see who this was?"

"No, I figured it was a farmer or someone dropping off a delivery," Horst said with a shrug. "I didn't get a good look. Most of the time, my paintings are from memory anyway."

Bev inspected the painting more closely, searching for a familiar cloak or dressing. "Was it a man or woman? Tall or short? Did they come inside the inn or keep walking? Have you seen them again?"

He shrugged, looking at the painting with a frown. "They were wearing a cloak over their head, so I didn't get a good look. Why?"

Bev plastered on a smile. "I'm sure Ida and Vellora would love to have this."

"Take it, please," he said. "I've got plenty more ideas now that I've got my beloved sibling nearby."

The rest of the art was packed into Horst's traveling bag. Even though the sun had long since set, the moon was high and bright, and Ramone *insisted* that their sibling come stay with them that night. Bev loaded them up with the remnants of the rosemary bread and triple-checked that Ramone didn't want to stay in the spare bedroom until morning.

"We have much to create," Ramone said with a smile. "And with any luck, my dear sibling will have a host of new material to bring to his master's home for the solstice."

"I already feel more inspired than I have in months," Horst replied. "Thank you, Bev, for everything you've done to heal this terrible rift between my sibling and me. You are truly a masterful host."

"I didn't do a thing," Bev said—and that was true. "But I'm glad to see you two happy."

Horst turned to go then stopped and came back to her. "Oh, I do remember one thing. That shadowy person had come from the farmlands to the west and returned that way."

Bev started. "They did?"

Horst nodded. "Must've been going far, because they were dressed to travel." He paused. "I hope that was helpful. If I remember anything else, I'll let you know."

Bev didn't have time to think too much about the new turn of events as Collin came up to stand next to her. He held two paintings, but couldn't stop staring at the one of himself.

"Art truly is magic," he whispered.

"How so?" Bev asked.

"Well, I was considering selling my lute after this week," he said. "But here... I look so happy playing my instrument. At peace. Whole, even. I don't think there's anything else in the world that could make me feel this way."

Bev gazed down at the painting, noting the way the light reflected in his eyes and the ease of his smile. "Horst is right. You shouldn't let one person's opinion get you down. Especially when it comes to art. It's all subjective, you know."

He nodded, watching the two siblings on the other side of the room. "I can't believe how quickly Wallace got them to make up. One minute, fighting like cats and dogs, the next, off on an artistic adventure in the snow together. How did he do it?"

"You'll have to ask the cleric," Bev said. "He's very persuasive when he wants to be, I suppose."

"But to be *so* persuasive," Collin said. "I'm eager to know how that's possible. Do you think he slipped something into their drinks?"

"If he did, I'm sure the siblings will wake up tomorrow and be at each other's throats," Bev said with a chuckle. "But they'll be in Ramone's house, not mine, so not quite my concern."

The bard nodded. "Have a good night, Bev. Hopefully, the snow melts in the morning."

"You know, every time I say that, I wake up with another inch on the ground."

CHAPTER SEVENTEEN

True to form, there *was* another inch on the ground in the morning—yet the weather had taken a decidedly warmer turn. If this kept up, then there was a good chance everyone could make their destinations by the solstice. Bev was in a fine mood as she started her morning chores before the sun even came up. After all, she needed to get a move on if she wanted to make it out to Herman's today.

You also need to give the butchers an update.

There was much she hadn't told them, including that Estera's regiment was hunting magic, the mysterious stranger in the painting going west, not to mention the Wersts' occupations. She didn't want to risk another incident of Vellora losing her cool, especially since Abigail was already so nervous about her.

But more importantly, Bev was no closer to pinpointing the culprit than when the first letter had arrived. One shadowy figure in a painting didn't make for a good clue—even if they'd come from the west, that could've been anyone. The inn was still full of suspects, each with a plausible motive. Though with that magic ring at their disposal, Wallace and Paul had certainly fallen low on Bev's list of suspects.

Speaking of, the cleric was the first one down the stairs that morning. He looked fairly green, and his face fell when Bev told him Allen hadn't arrived yet with breakfast.

"He'll be here soon," Bev said. "You're up early." *Considering the ale stench on your breath.*

"The early worm gets the bird," he said, absent-mindedly as he meandered over to the chairs in front of the fire and removed the cushion, running his hand along the bottom.

"Did you lose something?" Bev asked.

"Uh, well…" His face flushed. "Yeah, darnedest thing. I…uh…seem to have misplaced my ring."

"Misplaced?" Bev frowned. "When?"

"I'm not quite sure," he said. "My husband had gone to bed by the time we'd finished with the siblings, and Bernie and Collin were staying up by the fire to play games, so, of course, I joined them. Sometime…sometime, I must've misplaced it." He cleared his throat nervously. "We were so enthralled in conversation last night."

And probably drink, too. "Does anyone else know that it's—"

"No, no." His face screwed up in worry. "Can't believe I told *you* that. Must not have been in my right mind." He shook his head. "Sometimes, after I use it, I feel a bit…" He cleared his throat. "Cocky, you know."

Bev sighed. "If you're sure no one knows how special it is—"

"I am very sure."

"Then let me help you look for it," Bev said. "I'm sure it just fell out of your pocket."

Wallace grimaced like he'd rather not get up, but gingerly joined her rifling through the other chairs by the fire and checking under the table and between the planks on the floor. After a good search, they came up empty.

"I'm sure it'll turn up," Bev said, putting her hands on her hips. But the optimism was for Wallace only; she was fairly sure *someone* had taken it. Even not knowing it was magical, it was still a large, expensive-looking gem.

"Perhaps I'll head upstairs to check my room

again," Wallace said. "I appreciate your help." He walked toward the staircase, then paused and let out a small whimper, clutching his temple. "In a minute. Might need to sit down for a spell."

The front door opened and Allen came in with the breakfast biscuits, motioning to Bev to follow him into the kitchen after depositing the basket on the front counter.

"Here." He handed her a fragrant bag. "Your ginger finally arrived. The snow melted enough for my supplier to come in."

Bev opened the bag and inhaled, scenting the delicious root. "Thanks. Was that all you wanted to talk about?"

"Not at all," he said, lowering his voice. "I have news about the mysterious man who keeps coming into the shop and ordering baked goods."

Bev waved him off. "Oh, that's actually Horst Comely, Ramone's brother. We had this big reveal last night, and—"

"It's not. It's Jasper Klose. And if you hurry, he *just* left my shop and headed out of town."

~

Now, even though it was a little warmer, Bev wasn't eager to traipse through the snow for fun. But if Jasper was the one coming into town, *and* Horst said the shadowy figure had come and gone to the west, that was a bit too coincidental to ignore.

It didn't take her long to find the Middleburg resident, as his dark cloak was quite visible against the white snow, even in the dim light of the early morning.

"This is ridiculous," she whispered. "Should be going to Herman's house to check on his goats. Can't be following random townsfolk from Middleburg in the snow."

Yet she continued, something urging her to see this one through. At the very least, she'd be able to cross another suspect off her list.

"Bev?"

Bev froze mid-step and turned around. Grant appeared from behind a snow-covered tree, looking as if he'd been caught with his hand in the cookie jar.

"Grant," Bev said. "What are you doing out here? And so early?"

"I could ask you the same question," he said with a tight smile.

"I'm…" Bev glanced at Jasper, who was starting to grow smaller the longer she stood here. "Where is your cousin going?"

"Cousin?" He spun around, blinking in the direction Jasper had gone. He was still very clearly visible, but when Grant turned around, his face was blank. "What are you talking about?"

"Okay, Grant, don't play dumb with me," Bev

said. "Where is your cousin going?"

"I, uh…" The farmer rubbed the back of his neck. "I don't know what you're talking about. Jasper's back at my house, obviously."

Bev scoffed and walked around him.

"Bev, wait," Grant said, following her. "Look, nothing is going on. Jasper's out for a walk around town to stretch his legs, that's all."

"The town he hates?" Bev said, continuing to walk. "And he's not walking around town anymore."

"Well, he's headed back to my house."

"You live west. He's going north." Bev stopped, narrowing her gaze at him. "What are you trying to hide, Grant? Are you the ones threatening the Witzels?"

"Threatening the…" He blinked and there was honest confusion there. "Someone's threatening Ida and Vellora?"

Bev turned to keep walking. "Yes. And right now, you're acting cagey, and your cousin is acting even cagier. So what am I supposed to think about that?"

"I promise, Jasper's not doing anything to the Witzels. Sure, there's bad blood, but that's not… That's him being petty. He would never *threaten* anyone."

"I'll be the judge of that," Bev said. "Especially

if you tell me where he's going."

"I don't..." He sighed, almost defeated. "Fine. I don't know where he's going. To be honest, I kind of agree with you that he's been acting weird. He came with a giant bag he wouldn't let me look at. He keeps sneaking out of my house. I saw him in town yesterday. Why would he leave without telling me?"

"Allen says he stops in to get a pastry every day," Bev said. "Right around this time, too. It's not much of a stretch to believe he might be the one delivering these threatening letters."

Grant made a face. "That seems...out of character for him."

"Well, look. We're out here. He's right there. Why don't we find out where he's going so we can get some answers, hm?"

Grant didn't say much. Bev was a *bit* more suspicious of him than she'd been before, and she wasn't sure she should've revealed the blackmail letter, but she was tired, cold, and *grouchy*.

"Look, Bev, I didn't mean to lie," Grant said. "I'm worried about my cousin, you know? He's under a lot of pressure in Middleburg to keep things up. I hear the butcher shop had a rough year—another shop opened in town that stole some of our business."

"Would that pressure make him threaten Ida?"

"I don't think so," he said. "I mean, I *wouldn't* think so. It's about money."

"And that's what the letter writer wanted," Bev said. "Money."

Grant opened and closed his mouth, looking somewhat guilty. "I *hope* it's not him. If it is, you can rest assured I'll make sure he's punished for it."

"If it's him, I'll be delivering him to Sheriff Rustin," Bev said.

Grant sighed. "What if I told him to knock it off? Do we really have to get law enforcement involved? If Jasper gets arrested, that'll spell even more trouble for the butcher shop in Middleburg."

"Look, let's just…" Bev shook her head. She was too soft for this line of work. "Let's see where he's going first. Then we'll figure out what to do with him."

The houses had thinned out already, and all that was left was farmland and…

"Is he going into the dark forest?" Grant asked.

The dark forest was a thick patch of trees north of town—and no good had ever come from anyone going in there. Bev had only been in a situation like the one she was in now once before. Following a sketchy young man to see why he was acting strangely.

In that case, it had been Allen Mackey dealing

with a magical dealer called a barus. Would Bev see the creature again, and what could Jasper be bartering for? Hearing about his money troubles with the butcher shop was one clue, but was it the whole picture?

"I guess we're going to follow him and find out," Bev said.

The *only* nice thing she could say about it was that due to the thick tree canopy overhead, there wasn't much snow on the ground, so walking was a lot easier. It felt a little warmer, too, though the darkness didn't help. Bev could've used her glowing stick, but she couldn't walk all the way back to the inn to retrieve it. So she walked slowly, being sure of her feet before stepping, and holding on to whatever hanging branch or nearby trunk she could. The last time she'd been here, the brambles and leaves had cleared her a path. This time, they seemed to be asleep. Or perhaps whatever spirits inhabited the vines and branches had taken off for warmer climates.

Grant followed, his fearful gaze visible in the dappled light overhead. "Do you know where you're going?"

"Somewhat," Bev said. "I think it's up ahead."

The small clearing where Allen had met the barus now played host to Jasper. The scowling man checked his pocket watch and adjusted something large and bulky under his cloak. Bev and Grant knelt in the bushes a safe distance away, though still close enough to see and hear what was going on.

"What do you think he's waiting on?" Grant asked.

Bev shrugged but put her finger to her lips.

There was a rustling on the other side of the clearing, and a tall, severe-looking man walked out. His face was mangled, spotting a horrific-looking scar down his left cheek and disappearing under his shirt. He wore an impressive metal bangle around his left wrist that resembled a manacle without the chain.

"Well, it's about time you showed up," Jasper groused, pushing himself to stand. "I've been dragging myself here every day for half a week waiting for you."

"A *thousand* apologies," he said with a sneer. "Have you not noticed the snow on the ground? Makes it hard to get around."

Jasper growled, unfurling his cloak to reveal something large and almost egg-shaped, covered in red scales. Grant held his breath and shook his head, muttering to himself, but Bev was lost.

"Is that it?" the other man asked.

"Does it look like it's it?" Jasper said. "Do you have my money?"

"Well, I need to look at the egg to make sure it's

the real deal," he said, rubbing the thin mustache on his lips. "May I?"

"Show me you've got the gold first," Jasper said, shrugging his cloak back to reveal a large knife at his waist. "And don't try anything funny."

"Wouldn't dream of it," the other man said, inching forward as he put his hand inside his own cloak. He revealed a large bag of money that he put on the stump, the *clink* of the coins echoing in the silence.

Hesitant, Jasper handed the man the egg and began counting the coins greedily.

"Yes, this is a fine specimen," the man whispered, running his hands along the scales. "Worth the price, for sure."

"It wasn't easy to get," he said. "It's passed through a lot of hands from the mountains. I was lucky to get possession of it myself."

"I'm sure, I'm sure. And which hands gave it to you?"

Jasper gave him a look. "Don't you know? Freda Thurlow was the one who—"

"*Now!*" A third voice echoed from the clearing across from them and before Bev knew what was happening, ten uniformed soldiers appeared out of nowhere and pounced on Jasper. Bev's heart sank into her stomach as she recognized two of them—the soldier from the tea shop and…

"Good green earth, Estera, who taught you how to tie a rope?" the leader said. "Henry, fix that before he wriggles out of it?"

The soldier from the tea shop pushed Estera back, sending her onto her rear. She winced, but didn't say anything, scrambling back to her feet and looking like she wanted to be helpful, but at the same time, not garner the attention of her terrifying boss.

Jasper struggled against his bonds, calling the man a traitor and a saboteur, but the leader simply shrugged.

"You should know who you're dealing with," he said, scooping up the bag of coins and tucking the egg underneath his armpit. "And coming alone? That was a mistake, too."

"Where in the green earth did you even come from?" Jasper said, wriggling against the soldiers who had him bound. "There aren't supposed to be soldiers around here for miles."

"We heard tell of some illegal wyvern egg dealings and thought it was best to investigate." He leaned in close to Jasper. "And if you know of any other unsanctioned magic occurring around these parts, you might find yourself in jail a couple fewer days." He smiled. "Anyone other than Freda, who gave you up, so I can't give you any credit for that…"

He swallowed, and for a long moment, Bev held her breath, praying he'd say nothing about Ida or any of the other magical folks in town. She didn't know how much Grant might've told him, but he looked ready to say anything to save his own skin.

But to her relief, he shook his head. "I don't do the magic stuff, usually. The butcher shop's seen a bit of a hit with sales, and—"

"Such a shame," the man said, snapping his fingers. "Into the cart with him and back to camp. We'll see if he thinks of anything else along the way."

Grant covered his mouth, moving to help his cousin, but Bev shook her head. She didn't know much about these things, but it was clear Jasper had illegally obtained some kind of magical egg, had arranged a deal with an unknown buyer, and that buyer had sold him out to the queen's soldiers. That was the sort of thing that couldn't be talked out of.

They needed to leave before they, too, were spotted. She motioned behind her, but Grant shook his head, watching his cousin with a horrified face. But, finally, at Bev's insistence, he slunk silently away to follow her, and they slipped quietly back out toward the snowy realm beyond.

CHAPTER EIGHTEEN

"I can't believe what I just saw," Grant muttered to himself as they left the dark forest. "What in the world was Jasper thinking, dealing in dragon eggs like that?"

Bev didn't know what to say, because she had more pressing matters to worry about. It was one thing to say the soldiers had been venturing into the city to get warm and buy provisions. It was entirely another that they were setting up traps in the dark forest to capture magical dealers. And…very clearly *camping* much closer to Pigsend than Bev had thought.

Had Estera offered *that* bit of information to

anyone in the inn? Or was *she* the one sending the letters after all?

"Bev?" Grant had been talking with her. "Did you hear me?"

"Sorry. My mind's elsewhere," Bev said. "What did you say?"

"I asked if you...well, if you thought any less of me for that?" Grant said. "I swear, I didn't have a clue what Jasper was up to." He shook his head, shock still evident on his face. "Things must've been worse than I thought. Jasper would never... I mean, thieving and underhandedness is on the *other* side of..." He trailed off, giving Bev a sideways glance. "Sorry. Old habits, you know."

She sighed, shaking her head. "I'm worried, Grant."

"About Jasper—"

"No, as much as I feel for your cousin, he made his bed," Bev said. "I'm worried about the Witzels. Someone is keen on getting them in trouble, and I haven't a clue who it might be."

"If I can help in any way, let me know," he said.

Bev stopped, staring at him intently. "Did Jasper know about Ida's super strength?"

To her relief, Grant shook his head. "I only know because I've seen it around town. But it's not as if any of us really think it's...well, it's not something like illegal wyvern egg selling that could really get you in trouble."

Bev exhaled, some of the tension leaving her chest. A little reprieve. "I'm sorry he's in this situation. Hopefully, they don't keep him..." She didn't really want to say it. "Hopefully, he gets out unscathed and quickly."

Grant nodded, but Bev had a feeling they both knew the reality wasn't going to be as kind. She hoped Vellora and Ida wouldn't be so unlucky.

Bev returned to the inn, purposefully taking the long way to avoid the butchers. As long as she could, she'd delay the inevitable. So she set to making her bread, preparing her vegetables, anything to avoid crossing the street to put her meat order in for the day.

As she worked, she couldn't help but replay the scene in the forest—namely, Estera. She hadn't looked pleased to be there, but she was still a suspect. Especially after Vellora had threatened her, there was definitely reason for her to dislike the butchers. And clearly, she was able to make good on her threats with her magic-catching boss, whatever-his-name-was.

There was a knock at the door, and Wallace came into the kitchen, holding his hands nervously. "Bev, I hate to interrupt, but I need to speak with you about my...uh...missing item."

"Did you find it?" she asked, wiping her hands on her apron.

His smile faltered. "Er…no. I haven't. Turned over the entire downstairs, too. Honestly, I'm a bit…nervous about where it might've ended up. You know I'm not one to point fingers, but…" He shifted, perhaps hoping she would fill in the blanks. "Is there anything you can do? Maybe under the guise of tidying up, you could…"

"I can't search their rooms," Bev said matter-of-factly. "But we have a sheriff in town. We could pay him a visit, and—"

"Oh, law enforcement? Queen's folk?" He shifted. "I'm not sure if that's the best idea…"

"Why not?"

"Well, I don't think I have to remind you that the ring is…well…*special*." He toyed with his fingers, almost as if the ring was a phantom presence on his hand.

"Look, we don't have to tell Rustin all the details. He isn't very…" She considered her phrasing. "He's…well, for lack of a better word, a bit cozy in his rural job where he doesn't have to do much. In fact, he might not even do a good job with searching the inn." Bev shrugged. "But his presence might scare someone into coughing it up, at least. And that's, after all, what we're after, isn't it?"

Wallace nodded, looking a bit more relaxed. "So

he's not…he's not one of those magic-obsessed people?"

"If he was, he's been blind to all the magic happening around Pigsend," Bev said with a half-smile.

"Well, I suppose if you believe it wouldn't…" He cleared his throat. "I've just heard there are some of those…well, magic-obsessed soldiers nearby."

"Really?" Bev said, curious who told the cleric.

"Estera's regiment," he said. "I hear they aren't too far away."

Closer than you think. "What did you hear about them?" Bev asked, looking down at her knife to avoid looking too interested.

"Just that she worked for none other than Dag Flanigan," Wallace said. "One of the most dangerous magic hunters around. Notorious, in fact. The queen's favorite."

Bev swallowed. "Oh." She looked down at her knife again. "I'm sure they've moved on by now."

"I'm sure they haven't," Wallace said. "Estera said they were on the hunt for someone selling a wyvern egg in the forest north of here."

"She told you that?" She paused. "Of course she told you that. Suppose she didn't *mean* to tell you that, hm? Used a little magic to get you the information you needed?"

"Young Collin told me that she was a soldier, so

I needed to know if I needed to be worried about her," Wallace said.

"Did you?"

"No. She may belong to that regiment, but she's just an extra body. Very glad to be away from her boss." He again reached for the phantom ring. "I hope she got home. She really wanted to see her mother again."

Bev felt a little better about Estera, but not much. "What else did she say about why she was here?"

"Ah...well..." He chuckled, his fingers searching for the missing ring again. "It wasn't her, but Bernie mentioned he saw a soldier the other day in the same regiment. This one seemed a bit more... *professional*, so to speak. I'd hate for him to show up in town and hear about the missing ring." He paused, shaking his head firmly. "On second thought, I really don't think anyone took it intentionally. Probably not necessary to get the law involved." He took a step backward. "You know, maybe it's in my room. Let me search it again—"

"Wallace, if I catch you snooping in the other rooms, I'll have no choice but to turn you out," Bev said with a warning glance. "So either we tell Rustin, or you're going to have to drop it. It's your choice."

The cleric stared at her for a few minutes, indecision clear on his face. Finally, his shoulders dropped.

"Fine. We'll pay the sheriff a visit."

Bev *really* didn't want to go back out in the snow, but the sooner Rustin was involved, the better the chances the ring would turn up. Especially if the snow kept melting and the travelers decided to try their luck out on the roads. The front doors of the town hall were open—a good sign—and there was a light in Rustin's office, along with voices. Bev adjusted her cloak and walked the length of the room until she came to the sheriff's door, which was open.

"Rustin, we have—"

She stopped short, and beside her, Wallace sucked in a loud breath. Rustin was at his desk, but he wasn't alone. The soldier from the dark forest sat across from him, lounging as if he owned the place. Up close, he was as intimidating and terrifying, and the scar that ran down his cheek was even more terrifying.

Rustin noticed them standing there and his face broke into a bright smile. "Bev! Your ears must've been burning. I was talking about you. This is—"

"Dag Flanigan," the soldier said, turning to look at Bev. "Of the queen's special service."

Wallace took a step backward, and Bev didn't need his magic ring to feel the panic radiating off him.

She schooled her features. "Pleasure to meet you, Mr. Flanigan. I'm Bev, proprietor of the Weary Dragon Inn."

"So I hear," Dag replied. "And who is your friend?"

"Wallace Cordell. Clergyman," he said, a little more confidently than his face would suggest. "I'm also staying at the Weary Dragon. Bev and I were just…uh…out for a walk. I'd asked to see the town hall."

"Indeed," Bev said, hearing his unsaid request to *not* mention the missing ring. "What are you doing in town, Mr. Flanigan? Heck of a time to be traveling. Are you headed somewhere for the solstice?"

He chuckled. "With apologies to the clergyman, I don't really celebrate the solstice. Not when there's important work to be done for the queen."

"Dag and a few of his soldiers are passing through and will be in need of a place to stay this evening," Rustin said. "I told them there was always space at the Weary Dragon."

"Ah, not much these days, but I have a bed or two available," Bev said. "How many do you need?"

"Six," Flanigan said.

Bev rubbed her chin. "I could possibly swing six if I can convince a couple folks to share a room."

"I'm sure Bernie and Collin wouldn't mind sharing," Wallace said.

"We are members of the queen's service," Dag said with a chuckle. "They should be happy to give up their rooms."

Bev forced a smile. "Well, I'm not sure about *happy*, but—"

"Then it's settled. We'll be there this evening."

Bev stepped outside the town hall and frowned —the sun was gone behind thick gray clouds again and there was a threatening cold breeze. "Don't you dare."

The sky made no indication that it had heard her.

"Well, this is certainly...something," Wallace said, his voice full of nerves. "I suppose we'll have to put that ring business to rest for a moment, eh? Might be for the best that it's gone." There was a light sheen of sweat on his forehead, even in the chilly air. "Those sorts of things... They aren't looked on too kindly by the queen's people. I'd hate for them to...well, to make a mountain out of a molehill, you know."

"And they do like to do that," Bev said. "I still think we should at least mention it to Rustin. He doesn't have to know that it's magic, just—"

"No." It was the firmest, most serious she'd ever

heard him. "No, the ring is as good as lost now. In fact, maybe it's time for Paul and me to make our escape to Kaiser Tuckey's. It's been a touch warmer, the roads are probably not as bad. We can make it if we—"

"Whatever you want to do," Bev said. "It would certainly make it easier to house six soldiers."

Wallace didn't respond, and Bev felt guilty for being so blunt. But the Witzel Butchery was up ahead, and Bev would have to deliver *awful* news to Ida and Vellora and have nothing to say to soothe them. But she could put off the conversation with the butchers no longer. The Wersts' occupation was one thing, but the cadre of soldiers from the dark forest was an entirely different story.

"Aren't you coming?" Wallace asked, his hand on the front door to the inn.

"In a minute," Bev said. "I've got to get my meat order in for the day."

She held her breath and pushed open the front door. Both Ida and Vellora were there, but neither looked pleased. There was another letter sitting on their counter, and Bev let out a loud sigh.

The price is now 150 pieces of gold. Tonight. Or else.

"Tell me you've got a suspect," Ida said. "Please,

I need some good news."

Bev pinched the bridge of her nose. "I wish I could say I did," Bev said. "But I do have…news."

Vellora stopped working and joined her wife by the counter. "What is it?"

"Before I tell you, I need you to promise you won't go across the street and harass my guests. They're already on edge as it is."

"Do they have reason to be on edge?" Ida asked, crossing her arms over her chest.

"Well, there's a large butcher across the street who's already run off one person for working for the queen," Bev said. "Which spooked some of the others who also…uh…work for her."

"Clearly, not enough for them to leave," Vellora snapped.

"Who else works for the queen? Bernie?" Ida said. "He seemed off to me."

"No, it's actually the—Wait, before I tell you, I want your word that you'll leave them alone. I'm convinced they aren't responsible," Bev said.

Vellora sighed. "Fine. We won't do anything."

Ida nodded but didn't say anything.

"That sweet little family with the small children," Bev said. "The mom is a registrar in Sidence. One of the head registrars."

Bev watched Vellora carefully, looking for any sign the butcher was hiding something. But she wore the usual scowl and look of disdain when anything about the queen was mentioned.

"Is that all?" Ida said. "Why would a bureaucrat be threatening us?"

"I don't think she is," Bev said. "But Etheldra had a good point about registrars...namely that the kingside soldiers need to keep in touch with theirs at least once a year. Is it possible that..." Bev again watched Vellora. "That Vellora hasn't been keeping up with hers?"

Neither spoke for a moment. Vellora clicked her tongue as her knuckles went white. "I receive a letter from my investigator every year. I always respond. There is nothing there."

"I can vouch for that," Ida said with a nod. "Because she's in a bad mood for days after. But the letter does get sent."

Bev watched the two of them, torn between asking for proof and believing her dearest friends.

"Have you been investigating *me* instead of my wife?" Vellora asked. "Because I'm not the one... I haven't done anything wrong."

"Neither has Ida, but the letters aren't exactly *specific* about whose secrets they're threatening to expose." Bev took a breath to keep her temper from rising. "I'm on your side. But I need the facts—all of them."

The two butchers were silent for a moment

before Vellora grabbed her small pad of paper. "What's the meat order tonight?"

"Vellora."

"We've got some pork loin. I'll drop it off—" She paused. "I suppose I'll have *Ida* drop it off since I don't want to be accused of scaring anyone."

"Actually," Bev said with a wince, "there is one more thing."

She explained following Jasper Klose, and the soldiers in the dark forest, hating the way that Vellora's face went from red to white in a matter of moments. She and Ida both sucked in a deep breath when Bev got to the part about Dag Flanigan being in Rustin's office.

"So they're…they're very close," Ida whispered. "The blackmailer must've known that."

Bev nodded. "And they're about to be a lot closer because they're…uh…staying at the inn tonight."

It became so quiet, Bev could hear the anger ticking higher in Vellora's mind.

"I wanted to give you a heads up," Bev said, inching backward toward the door. "Just in case, you know. I don't expect them to stay very long."

"How many?" Ida asked softly.

"Six," Bev said. "Including…well, including Estera, so Vellora, you might want to…"

The butcher let out a grunt of anger and

stormed up the stairs loudly. Bev winced as the upstairs door slammed so loudly that the windows rattled.

"I'm sorry," Bev said softly.

"Are you?" Ida asked, her eyes filling with tears. "You come in here and act like *we're* the ones under investigation. And now you're giving quarter to the very people who could haul us off in chains!"

Bev tilted her head. "What would you have me do? Deny them? That would look suspicious."

"I want you to find out who's blackmailing us," Ida said, wiping her cheeks. "Look, I've got to carve up more meat for these soldiers who'll likely arrest us in the morning. I assume that's really why you came—"

"Ida, don't be—"

"I think it's best you leave," Ida said softly, turning to follow her wife up the stairs. "I'll drop the meat off later today."

CHAPTER NINETEEN

Bev crossed the street and went through the kitchen door, guilt weighing heavily on her shoulders. She'd never so much as uttered a cross word with the butchers, let alone been kicked out of their shop. They had every right to be angry with her, which made things all the more upsetting for Bev.

Biscuit was waiting for her in the kitchen, seeming to understand that she was in a mood, so he nuzzled her leg then went back to sleep. She chopped vegetables, checked on her bread, and tidied up as she went. Normally, these kinds of mundane tasks got her mind moving, considering the problem from new angles. But all she could think about were the tears in Ida's eyes, and how disappointed both butchers were in her.

Thud.

Bev stopped short, her gaze lifting to the ceiling. Biscuit lifted his head to sniff, turning toward the kitchen door.

"What d'ya reckon that was?" Bev asked, wiping her hands on her apron. "The boys getting into trouble?"

She fell silent as the sound of raised voices echoed down from above. She rolled her eyes and took off her apron, leaving it on the table as she hurried out into the main room. She took the stairs two by two until she came upon the scene: Collin and Bernie were arguing with Wallace, and someone's traveling pack had been spilled onto the floor.

"What in the... What's going on here?" Bev said.

"I was *helping* Collin move his things into Bernie's room," Wallace said. "Since we're expecting Mr. Flanigan and his soldiers soon."

"More like *dumped* my things on the floor," Collin said with a huff as he bent down. "And then *accused* me of theft!"

"Wallace," Bev said, looking at the clergyman.

"First of all, his bag slipped out of my hand,"

Wallace said, though from the look on his face, the cleric wasn't used to lying. "Second, I didn't *accuse* anyone of anything. I merely *asked* if he might've seen my ring among his items."

"He flat-out asked if I'd stolen it!" Collin said. "Said it made sense, considering that I didn't have any other skills to speak of. I don't see why he's not accusing Bernie of stealing it. He's as lacking in a real job as I am!"

"Don't bring me into this!" Bernie said, holding up his hand. "I don't like jewelry."

"A likely story," Collin said with a sneer. "And you want me to bunk with him tonight? I'd rather —"

"You are, of course, all welcome to leave," Bev said, lightly. "No one's keeping you here."

"They can't!" Wallace said. "Not until I've found my ring."

"Then I suggest you go back to the sheriff's office and file an official report," Bev said. "In the meantime, Collin, Bernie: since you're being asked to move rooms, tonight's on the house. Wallace, if you can't keep your accusations to yourself, I'm going to have to ask *you* to leave."

The three men quieted, looking at each other with more animosity than Bev had seen from any of them.

"Now, why don't we all take a collective breath,"

Bev said. "Wallace, we'll search for your ring. I'm sure Bernie and Collin would be *happy* to let you look in their things. After all, if there's nothing to hide, there's nothing to be worried about, hm?"

"I didn't take your stupid ring," Collin said, gathering the shirts and stuffing them back in the bag before marching into Bernie's room.

Bernie shrugged. "You're welcome to look in my things as well. I have nothing to hide."

"No one will be searching anything," Bev said. "May I speak with Wallace alone?"

Bernie disappeared into the room, leaving Bev and Wallace out in the hall.

"Wallace, what did I say about searching their rooms?" Bev said, with an exhausted sigh. "I've half a mind to kick you and your husband out. You keep talking about leaving anyway.

The cleric hung his head. "I'm sorry. I was just hoping to get it back before... But maybe Paul won't notice it's missing. He'd be furious at me for losing such an expensive item."

"I'm sure he'd notice..." Bev stopped, looking at him. "Wallace, does your husband know the ring is *special*?"

"Not exactly." He glanced around and lowered his voice. "You know, he's a wonderful man, but he's so...uh...well, *focused* on the business side of things. I feared if I told him...he might ask me to well, use it in ways I didn't quite agree with. Wanting me to persuade people to give us discounts, that sort of thing. As a rule, I don't tell people what the ring could do."

Bev had a hard time believing that, considering how easily the information had come out of him. "I see."

"He's a good man, I promise. Just...a bit anxious. Worried about money because he never had any growing up—"

"Did your ring tell you that?" Bev asked, tilting her head.

He lowered his hands helplessly. "I'm not a bad person, Bev."

"I don't think you are, Wallace. But you need to shape up. We have a cohort of soldiers arriving soon, and I don't want to give them *any* reason to believe *any* of us need to be led away in handcuffs." Bev sighed, thinking of the Witzels. "So let's just be on our best behavior tonight, and everyone can be on their way in the morning."

Bev returned to the kitchen and exhaled loudly. Biscuit was still by the hearth, watching her intently. She narrowed her gaze at the laelaps.

"*You* didn't take Wallace's ring, did you?" Bev asked.

He let out a low ruff.

"I'm going to believe that's a no," she said with a sigh. "But if you did, be a lamb and return it, will you?"

Biscuit curled into a ball and fell back asleep.

Bev went back to work on dinner, but the hour was growing late, and there was still no sign of Ida. Bev wondered if the butchers had decided *against* filling her order, perhaps out of spite, but she wasn't brave enough to venture across the street again. She could get dinner made in under an hour if needed (it wouldn't be her best, but it would be edible), but she would need that meat.

Finally, at just past four-thirty, the back door opened and Ida walked in carrying the promised food.

"Ida, I'm so glad that—" Bev stopped, registering the tears on Ida's face. "What is it?"

"We've..." She glanced around as she put the meat on the counter. "I can't stay long, or else Vel will know something's up."

"What is it?" Bev asked, walking up to her. "What happened? Another letter?"

"Yes and..." Ida swallowed. "Yes and no. After you left, Vel got... Well, she wanted to..." Ida ran a nervous hand through her hair. "Vel decided it was time to respond. So she wrote a note and told the blackmailer that we'd... Well, we'd meet them at Herman's house with the money. And they left this."

Monday's house it is. 9 o'clock tonight. Don't try anything funny or I'll have Dag Flanigan at your door.

"Ida, you can't possibly be thinking of paying them," Bev said. "And why in the world did Vellora want to meet him at Herman's house?"

"Because it's empty," Ida said. "Because Vellora isn't *planning* on paying them." Ida bit her lip, her eyes filling with tears. "She's planning on…well, *snuffing out* whoever it is. That's why we agreed to meet them at Herman's house. Vel said… She said that it would muffle any screams."

Bev put her hands to her mouth. "Ida, you can't let her—"

"That's why I'm here," Ida said, clearing her throat. "Vellora thinks we don't have a choice but to fight him, but we do," Ida said, throwing her shoulders back. "If you still have it, can I get the gold I paid you for the p-party?" Her voice cracked as a single tear leaked down her cheek. "I guess we'll have to cancel it, but…but that's all right."

Bev watched her for a long time, then nodded sadly, crossing the kitchen to retrieve the gold satchel Ida had given her a few days before. She gave it to Ida wordlessly, wishing she had something—anything—that might change her mind.

"Thank you," Ida said, inhaling. "Hopefully, with this, I can talk some sense into my wife. Then we can pay him and he'll just...he'll just leave us alone."

Bev watched helplessly as Ida left her in the silent kitchen. Mechanically, she turned to prepare the meat, her mind spinning as she ran through her list of suspects for what felt like the millionth time. Collin, Bernie, Paul, Wallace—

No, not Paul and Wallace, she corrected herself. Not with that magic ring.

So Collin and Bernie, then. And maybe Estera, too.

Whoever the culprit was, the butchers were going to find out tonight.

Biscuit let out a low bark, and the front door to the inn scraped open. The soldiers had arrived.

"All right, Bev," she muttered to herself. "Toughen up. The butchers will be fine. A bit lighter on gold, but they'll manage. Tomorrow, everyone will leave, and things will go back to normal."

But even as she said the words, a disappointing weight settled in her stomach. Still, she plastered on her best smile as she ventured out to greet her guests.

Flanigan stood at the front desk, that jagged scar standing out like a sore thumb. Behind him, Bev counted the five soldiers he'd promised, including

Henry from the tea shop and young Estera, who was all but hiding behind the rest of them, perhaps not wanting to be noticed.

"Welcome to the Weary Dragon," Bev said, meeting them at the front desk. "Or welcome back, I should say. Glad to see you again, Estera."

"Oh? You know each other?" Dag asked, glancing at his charge. "You didn't mention you'd been in town."

"I stayed here briefly," Estera said. "The snow, you know. Got caught."

"She left in such a hurry," Bev replied, glancing between the soldier and her commander to see if Estera had told Dag about *why* she'd departed so quickly.

"Just eager to see my mom," Estera said, with a meaningful look.

"And did you get to see her?" Bev asked.

"Unfortunately, no," Estera said. "No, I ran into… And um…" Her face flushed. "Anyway. I'm back at work."

"That's a shame. Hopefully, you'll get to go home soon." She turned to Dag, who was watching the exchange with interest. "Mr. Flanigan, I was able to consolidate some guests to find you six beds in three rooms. Just the one night, correct?"

Dag nodded. "Unless there's a pressing need for us to stay longer."

"Can't imagine you'd find one." Bev scrawled *Queen's Soldiers* on rooms two, four, and five. "That'll be three gold pieces."

He placed the money down on the table. "I assume dinner will be served soon?"

Bev nodded and handed them their keys. "Yes, of course. I'm just about to put it in the oven. Just got the meat delivered from the butcher, so it should be about an hour before it's ready."

He grunted in affirmation, then divided the keys amongst the soldiers, and all of them, save Estera, marched upstairs.

"Butchers, huh?" she said, twisting her hands. "Hope you didn't mention I was back. Would hate to see them... Well, would hate for that big one to find out who I work for."

"I would as well," Bev said. "But I am happy to see that you're safe. The lot of us were worried about you in all this weather."

She puffed out her chest. "No need. Been freezing my butt off in a tent instead of sleeping in my own bed. But it's fine. My mom probably wasn't looking forward to seeing me anyway."

"So you've been in town this whole time?" Bev asked, trying to avoid sounding suspicious.

"I wouldn't say *in town*," she said, making a face. "If you call sleeping in that forest north of here *in town*."

"No, can't say I would," Bev said. "Well, the fire's warm down here, and if you're still chilled, I'd be happy to make you a cup of tea. It won't be the same as your mom's but—"

"Thanks." She gave the briefest of smiles. "I'm going to go upstairs and rest. Been a busy day. Busy day tomorrow, too, I'd bet."

Bev nodded as the soldier dashed up the stairs. Estera's return added yet another wrinkle to an already complicated picture. Bev had an inn full of suspects, and her time was running out to identify the real culprit.

CHAPTER TWENTY

With Bev's attention on anything but dinner, it was nothing short of a miracle that it came out edible.

She plated the meal and brought it out into the front room, finding several of those suspects seated around a table enjoying a pint together. Estera, back on the list after a long absence, seemed to be the most quiet. Collin was talking with Bernie and Paul. Wallace was nowhere to be found, but at least those at the table seemed to be tolerating each other's company.

"Looks delicious, Bev," Bernie said, grabbing a plate.

"Agreed," Collin said. "Just a shame it'll be our last meal here."

"Oh?" Bev looked around. "Everyone planning on leaving tomorrow?"

Paul sidled up next to Collin with an uncharacteristically happy look on his face. "Yes. Estera said the roads look good."

"Oh, you spoke with her?" Bev said, trying to keep her tone light when she felt so down. "She seems sad to be back here. Shame she didn't make it home."

"And if you talk to her, she's been having a *rough* go of it," Collin said with a chuckle. "Seems to blame the butchers for all her problems."

Bev gave a thin smile. "Hopefully, she won't be too averse to eating their meat, then."

"I certainly will be happy to eat something else," Paul said. Then, perhaps recognizing that he'd spoken a little *too* plainly, he cleared his throat. "Not that I haven't enjoyed the meals here. Just eager to get to Kaiser Tuckey's. I hear he makes quite the solstice feast."

"Surprised you two will be leaving," Bev said. "Did Wallace find his ring?"

"His ring?" Paul frowned. "Did he misplace it?"

"You didn't hear the commotion earlier?" Bev asked. "There was some...er...discussion about where it might've run off too."

"No, I was out for a walk," Paul said, putting down his plate. He looked more upset than Bev would've guessed. "I'll be right back. I need to talk with Wallace."

He left his plate on the table and took to the stairs, leaving Bev to wonder what Wallace had told his husband about the ring's abilities.

"Don't worry, Bev," Bernie said with a smile, as he took Paul's place in front of her. "I don't have any plans of leaving. Might just stay until the spring at this rate."

"The price will go back up once the snow melts," Bev said, a little grumpily.

Bernie frowned and returned to the table, and Bev felt bad for taking her frustrations out on him. But her guilt was short-lived, as the soldiers emerged from the upstairs, led by Flanigan and trailed by Estera. Bev plastered on her nicest expression as each walked by, murmuring their thanks and filling their plate.

Then Peter and Pascal came bounding down the stairs, racing each other with loud squeals of joy. Byron came after, exasperatedly telling them to slow down, then Abigail made her appearance, with the baby strapped to her. Estera took the opportunity to rush to the table of soldiers and purposefully avoid Bev's gaze as the family's noise proved to be a distraction to everyone.

Abigail's face brightened when she saw Flanigan, and she approached him with shoulders thrown back and her hand extended.

"Mr. Flanigan, I've heard a lot about you. Abigail Werst, registrar from Sidence. It's a pleasure to finally meet you."

Bev doubted Flanigan would shake her hand with the way he was looking at her, but perhaps Abigail's position was high enough to demand respect as he accepted the gesture.

"What are you doing this far from home?" Flanigan asked, glancing at the rest of her family. "And with this many...children?"

"They're mine," she said with a soft smile. "Got trapped here by the snow, as did everyone else, I'd wager. Surprised to see you traveling in all this muck."

"We have an important mission to carry out," he said, his sharp gaze landing on Collin, Wallace, and Bernie as if looking for magic on them. "The queen's demands wait for no one."

"And what does the queen need with this small town?" Abigail asked, a little incredulously.

"We've been told there might be something worth looking into," Dag said, his face a mask. "This town's getting something of a reputation. First, sinkholes start forming all over the place. Then, a Harvest Festival with all manner of *curiosities*."

Bev bristled—the sinkholes were caused by another group of queen's soldiers and the Harvest Festival *curiosities* were due to Renault or Claude searching for magic. Neither one was the fault of the town. But she kept her mouth shut. She was more concerned about what these soldiers had been told.

"Well, I think you'll find it's a quiet sort of town," Wallace said, rising quickly, his plate still half-full. "But my husband and I will be leaving in the morning, so I'm going to go to bed." He laughed nervously. "Have a lovely evening, everyone."

Bev took his plate as he approached. "Everything all right, Wallace?"

"Oh, sure, sure." He looked to be sweating again. "Just need to get to bed. I'm sure Paul wants to get out first thing so we can get set up for the solstice tomorrow."

"Are you sure you want to leave without finding your ring?" Bev asked.

He jumped as if the mere mention of the ring was enough to send him to the gallows. "I'd like to stay, but unfortunately, I've been overruled by Paul. He would rather freeze to death than miss out on coin, you know."

He glanced over his shoulder to where his husband was sitting, finishing his meal. Paul, at least, didn't seem to be in a hurry to leave the soldiers. But then again, he didn't know his husband had been carrying a ring that could have...

Bev started. She'd all but dismissed Wallace as a suspect, but *Paul?* If he didn't know his husband carried magic, then perhaps *he* could be the blackmailer.

"Mm." She tilted her head. "He said he was out for a walk earlier. Do you know where he went?"

"No, can't say I do. He does like to get out and stretch his legs. I think he keeps going out of town to check the roads." He took a step back, inching toward the stairwell. "If I don't see you in the morning, then thank you for everything."

Bev waved as he hightailed it up the stairs, her suspicions raised even further. Was Wallace in on the blackmail, nervous that his husband was threatening to expose innocent magical users when he, himself, was one? Or were his nerves purely because of the soldiers sleeping in the next room over, and he was oblivious to his husband's machinations?

Wallace scurried up the stairs, and it seemed only Bev was interested in his hasty departure. Abigail was still chatting with Flanigan, who looked like he wanted to escape, while Byron was settling the boys at the table. The other soldiers ate silently, watching their boss with a wary eye. At the other table, Collin and Bernie were engrossed in conversation and Paul was reading his book.

Paul. Was it her imagination, or was he glancing at the clock? Counting down until nine until he'd leave for Herman's house to get his gold?

Just as she had that thought, he rose and brought his plate to Bev. "Another excellent meal. Thank you."

"If Wallace is to be believed, you two will be headed out early," Bev said, struggling to keep her tone friendly as she scrutinized the cleric's husband carefully.

"As early as possible."

"Just a shame Wallace lost his ring," Bev said. "It seemed to be quite expensive."

"Gaudy thing." Paul rolled his eyes. "He won it in a card game, of all things, and I told him I thought it was ugly, but he insisted on keeping it. Better off gone, if you ask me. Besides that, we'll be flush with gold tomorrow—"

"Oh?" Bev said, nearly jumping across the front desk. "Why's that?"

"The solstice?" he said with a quirked brow. "Goodness, have I done something wrong? You're looking at me as if I've taken your dog."

Bev took a breath. "Sorry, just… Well, have a good night. Safe travels in the morning if I don't see you."

~

As the minutes ticked on, the diners finished their meal and ascended up the stairs until the only ones left were Estera, Bernie, and Collin, who had huddled around the fire to talk. Bev took the dirty dishes to the kitchen, but propped the door open and told Biscuit to let her know if anyone came or went. The laelaps stretched out by the door, keeping his golden eyes on the living room.

Bev cleaned the plates, pots, and pans, her attention on Biscuit and the clock. Had the Witzels left yet? Had Ida convinced Vellora to just pay the blackmailer and not the violent alternative?

She was so lost in thought she almost didn't hear the low *ruff* that came from Biscuit. Quickly, she threw down the plate she was scrubbing and wiped her hands on her apron. But before she could reach the door, Collin walked through, looking pleased with himself.

"Collin, excuse me," Bev said.

"I just wanted to pay you for the night," Collin said, stepping in front of her with his usual smile. "The full amount, I might add."

"That's great, I—" She stopped. "Where did you get money?"

"Took a job," he said. "And you'll be so proud of me, I got the coin up front this time."

"What kind of job?" Bev asked as Biscuit nuzzled the back of her calf. "And from who?"

"Well, I can't say," he said with a chuckle. "But it was a nice chunk of change, so to speak. I don't even have to go to Kaiser Tuckey's anymore. I'm set up for the season."

Biscuit's nose was more insistent, but Bev ignored him for the moment. She glanced at the clock—half past eight. "Collin, who paid you? It's important."

"Oh, *very*." He chuckled, reaching into his pocket to jingle the coins. "But I can't say. Part of the money was to make sure that I kept my mouth shut. Unless, of course, he doesn't come back by ten o'clock, then I'm to alert the soldiers."

"*Who* doesn't come back?" Bev said. "And from where?"

But he just wore his smug smile. "Easiest money I've ever made, I tell you. Just—"

"*Collin!*" Bev barked as Biscuit nipped the back of her leg. "I need to know what's going on. My friends are in trouble, and I have to go—"

"I'll say," Collin said, pulling out two gold coins to inspect them. "Estera said those butchers are going to regret threatening her. She said she's hoping that their arrest tomorrow will get her leave granted again—"

Bev pushed past him to the front room. Only Estera remained, sitting at the table and looking innocent. So if it wasn't her sending the letters…

"Estera, where is Paul?" Bev demanded.

"No idea," she said. "I—"

Bev ran past her, grabbing her cloak, and rushed out the door.

There were a pair of footprints in the snow leading away from the inn, joined by another two sets of footprints that came from the Witzels' house. Biscuit was at her heels, but Bev turned before she was two steps out the door and knelt to pet him on the head. "Listen, the snow is still too much for you, little guy. I want you to wait for me at the inn. If I don't come back by midnight, you need to fetch Allen and get him to find Sheriff Rustin, okay?"

The dog stared blankly at her, but he was smarter than he looked as he walked through the back door and into the kitchen. Bev closed the door behind her, wishing it was possible to bring him, but not wanting him to freeze to death in the still calf-high snow. The snow had melted during the warmth of the day, but was freezing again, making for a slippery walk.

The scenario was coming together in her mind. Paul, knowing that there might be a trap waiting for him at Herman Monday's house, had enlisted Collin to alert the soldiers if he didn't come back at a reasonable time. But he wasn't just going to take the money—he was going to alert the soldiers to

Ida's magic, too, so they'd be arrested even though they'd paid Paul his money.

Paul, whose own husband had been using magic all this time. Paul, who was so miserly he'd blackmail a pair of butchers instead of earning an honest day's living. Paul, who was *so eager* to leave in the morning.

Bev had run out the door without much of a plan, but as Herman's house drew closer, she hoped she might see the butchers and warn them, then talk with Paul herself. Or something.

Herman's house was in plain view ahead, and there was a light on inside. Bev held her breath and followed the footprints that led right to the front door. Instead of going inside, Bev knelt by the window. Ida and Vellora were there, along with a sack of money on the floor. They were talking with one another, looking sick as they kept glancing at the clock. Five until nine.

Bev knelt on the deck, using her knife to pry open the pane and let their voices filter through.

"We should go," Ida said. "The money's here."

"I want to see his face," Vellora said. "Or her face. Whoever it might be."

"You *promised*," Ida said. "No violence."

"I'm not going to *hurt* them." But Vellora didn't look like she meant it. "Just want to talk."

"I say we go. What if us being here scares them

off?"

"It won't."

Bev nearly fell backward as a decidedly *different* voice than she'd been expecting emerged from the shadows.

Chapter Twenty~One

It was *Bernie*, not Paul, who stepped into the light, watching Vellora and Ida with a greedy expression. "I'm honestly surprised you came. You seem more the kind to run with your tail between your legs."

"Who are you?" Vellora demanded. "And what do you want from us?"

"Your gold, obviously."

"But why?" Vellora said. "My wife—"

"Your wife? What does she have to do with anything?" Bernie turned to Ida. "Was she in the war, too?"

Vellora and Ida shared a look of surprise. "It

was...*me* you were blackmailing?" Vellora said.

He tilted his head, almost amused. "Well, most soldiers who fought in the Battle of Eriwall carry the guilt so heavily on their shoulders that even the mention of a crime sends them to their knees."

Vellora straightened. "How did you..."

"What's that?" Ida asked, looking at her wife.

"Oh, it was a nasty business. In a desperate attempt to win, kingside soldiers did some...well, it's not right for polite company. But suffice to say that although they won, the cost was..."

Vellora's face was growing darker by the moment, but not from anger...from shame. Her fists were clenched together as she stared at the ground.

"Okay, fine. She was in a nasty battle," Ida said, putting a comforting hand on her wife's shoulder. "But all those battles...it was forgiven. Vellora filled out the paperwork—fills it out every year, in fact, and sends it to her registrar like she's supposed to." Ida narrowed her gaze. "Unless that witch of a queen has changed her own rules again."

"Oh, this thing?" Bernie pulled out a small piece of paper with writing on it. Bev couldn't tell what it was from this distance, but, based on the way Vellora's eyes widened in shock, she could guess.

"That's my... How did you get that?" Vellora asked. "It's supposed to be with my file in

Groitown..." Her mouth fell open. "You're my registrar, aren't you?"

He nodded with a sly grin. "I am. And it *turns* out your card wasn't ever completed, and you've been ignoring our letters," he said, pulling out a different card, one that had much less writing on it. "Or maybe you've been responding dutifully. It all depends on what's in that sack."

Bev huffed angrily. *What a racket!*

"That can't be...?" Ida said to Vellora with a shake of her head. "Surely, there's more than one person who can make a form official?"

"Just me, unfortunately. Quite a loophole, isn't it?" He cracked a smile. "My bosses have far too many soldiers to keep track of each individual one. And all the way out here...well, let's say as long as I keep sending back letters, they don't question." He paused. "It's common for soldiers to disappear, you know. Lots skipped town, tried to hide who they were, changed their name...from Gekkert to Witzel, for example."

"I got married," Vellora said through gritted teeth.

"And to be honest, for most of those who were in the battle, the threat of exposing the secrets is enough to goad people into coughing up their gold. Nobody wants their loved ones to know what a *monster* they really are." He wagged his brows.

"Usually don't have to resort to faking their registration card." He paused, thinking. "But you really didn't suspect... You thought your wife was the target?" His beady-eyed gaze turned to Ida. "What secrets does she have?"

Bev started. *Bernie doesn't know about Ida's magical strength?*

Vellora took a step forward. "I could break your bones."

"You could, I'm sure," he said. "But I've asked my dear friend Collin back at the inn to send Dag Flanigan and the others to arrest you and your wife if I'm not back by ten. Paid him the money he was expecting to get from his gig at Kaiser Tuckey's house, too."

"On what charges?" Ida asked. "What business does a magical hunter have with a wayward soldier?

Bev was curious, too.

"You don't know about Flanigan, do you?" He cracked a smile. "Any other soldier, sure. He'd ignore it like so many. But the Battle of Eriwall is personal for him. He fought there, you know. Lost nearly his entire regiment. That scar on his face? That's courtesy of the king's magic wielders. Once I tell him who you are, he'll be more than happy to see you in handcuffs. Especially after what you did to *poor* Estera."

Neither butcher responded.

"I must say, I thought you might get off the hook, what with all this snow—I was sure Flanigan and his regiment had moved on. How *fortuitous* that they decided to stay at the Weary Dragon instead."

"How did you even know he was nearby?" Ida asked.

"Estera told me," he said. "Poor thing was as squeamish as a worm, but she was easy to get talking once she had a pint in her. Told me *all* about Dag and his soldiers staying north of town, and how she'd *only* gotten permission to leave, but she was *so nervous* that they'd be coming into Pigsend, and her leave would be canceled." He chuckled. "And thanks to you, that happened."

Those butchers are going to regret threatening her. She said she's hoping that their arrest tomorrow will get her leave granted again.

But of course, Bernie didn't offer up that little piece of information. Bev could have throttled him.

"Now if you don't mind, I'm going to take my money and—" He picked up the bag, frowning. "You better not have shorted me."

Ida swallowed. Bev recognized the satchel that had the solstice party gold in it—only fifty gold coins. And it didn't look to be any more full.

"This is a dangerous game you're playing," he said, reaching into his pocket.

Bev held her breath as Ida grabbed Vellora's arm,

but Bernie just pulled out something small. Red.

Wallace's ring!

He slipped it on his finger and began to twist it. "Now, I'm not eager to cause trouble, and you two will be as good as arrested tomorrow. So why don't you take me back to your butcher shop and give me the rest of the gold, eh?" He glanced at Ida. "It's under your bed, isn't it? The rainy day fund. You were hoping to surprise Vellora with a trip back to her hometown, weren't you?"

To Bev's horror, Ida nodded.

"Probably not the best idea, considering Vellora's family doesn't want to see her after the atrocities she committed," Bernie said, twisting the ring more. He paused and smiled at it. "This thing is going to come in handy, isn't it?"

Bev balled her fists and stepped away from the window. She had to do…something, but she wasn't sure what she needed to do.

But first, she needed to get to the inn before Bernie did.

Bev burst into the front room of the Weary Dragon, heaving gasping breaths as she bent over. Biscuit trotted to her, and she patted him on the head.

"I'm okay," she said.

"Bev, goodness!" Collin came to stand next to

her. "What's wrong?"

"Where's Estera?" Bev said, straightening with some effort. "It's important."

"What is it?" The young soldier was seated by the fire, her wide eyes innocent. "What's wrong?"

"Did Bernie promise you something?" Bev said.

"Well, he certainly—" Collin began, puffing out his chest.

"Not talking to you," Bev snapped, quieting the bard immediately. "Estera. This is very important. Did he tell you that he could get your leave granted if you told Dag about someone in town?"

She toyed with her fingers nervously. "M-maybe he did. What's it to you?"

"Because you don't want to send innocent people to jail, do you?" Bev asked.

"Innocent?" The soldier rose, her face turning blotchy. "That woman nearly *killed* me! She's lucky I didn't mention it to… Well, it's not… I'm not supposed to be throttled by civilians." She cleared her throat. "But I didn't forget! I'm going to tell Dag about it in the morning."

"About *what*?" Bev pressed. "Vellora's missing registration card?"

"Yes, of course. What else could there be?"

Bev ran her hand over her hair. "Bernie is blackmailing the butchers, Estera. He's Vellora's registrar, but he's threatening to lie about her

272

paperwork unless she pays him 150 gold coins. But you're going to see to it that they're arrested anyway."

"That's impossible." Abigail's voice rang out from above. She wore her dressing gown, but the baby was fussing in her arms as she walked down the stairs. "*Bernie* is a registrar?"

Bev nodded, a glimmer of hope in her chest. "Yes. Or…what is it? An investigator?" She took a step toward Abigail. "He said he's the only one who can certify a soldier's card." She took a breath. "Tell me that's not how that works?"

Abigail adjusted the fussing baby in her arms, a nervous look on her face. "Well, I can't say for sure what happens in other districts. Some investigators are given much more leeway than others. But… but surely that isn't the case here. There must be a misunderstanding." She looked around. "Where is Bernie, anyway?"

"Walking back from Herman Monday's house with the Witzels," Bev said. "Aiming to get the rest of his gold."

"Look, I don't know what Bernie's doing or not doing, but those butchers are just getting what's coming to them," Estera said, turning to walk toward the stairs. "I'm going to bed. Have a long journey in the morning."

"So you've already told Dag about the butchers,

then?" Bev said, feeling defeated. "Gotten your leave approved?"

"N-no, not yet," Estera said. "But I'm sure that in the morning, he'll be happy to hear—"

"And you're sure he'll grant you leave with just a soldier who didn't finish their paperwork?" Bev asked, getting an idea. "What if...what if you were to find something else? Something magical?"

She paused on the bottom step. "Go on."

"Bernie has a ring," Bev said. "One—

Collin perked up again. "Oh, he took Wallace's —"

"Collin, I will pay *you* one gold coin to keep quiet the rest of the night," Bev snapped.

The bard quieted immediately.

"This ring has the power to read minds and influence them, too," Bev said. "I saw him use it on the butchers."

Estera turned around. "Really?"

"Really." Bev took a step forward. "Now, I know that Dag might've fought some battles, but his main charge is to hunt down magic, right? So if you really want to ensure you get home, go get your boss and tell him there's a magical ring next door at the butcher shop."

Flanigan didn't look pleased to be roused, especially by Estera. Bev only heard snippets of the conversation, but she was getting the distinct impression that Flanigan would rather any other soldier be on his team, but he was stuck with Estera.

"So what is this nonsense?" he asked, roughly pulling on his coat. "Something about a butcher?"

"There's a man who's trying to extort the butchers next door," Bev said. "He has a magical ring that—"

"*Magical* ring?" The commotion had woken Wallace and Paul, the latter looking at his husband incredulously.

"Y-yes," Bev said, as Wallace looked stricken. "*Bernie* has a magic ring. And if we hurry, we can catch him in the act."

It was a larger group than Bev would've liked. Flanigan, Estera, Abigail, Collin, Wallace, and Paul all clamored across the slushy street to the butcher shop. The light was on in the front, illuminating Bernie and Vellora. Ida was walking down the stairs with another gold satchel in hand.

Bev rushed through the front door, the group following a bit slower behind her, and Bernie turned suddenly as the room filled with people.

"What in the…" He met Bev's gaze, and wheels began turning. "O-oh… I'm so glad you're here! These butchers have threatened me, kept me here unless I pay them money!" He pointed to the sack of gold in Ida's hands. "This is all I have left! They took it!"

"That's the Witzels' money," Bev said. "Dag—"

"I saw the butchers threatening him," Collin said, pointing his finger at Vellora. "Yesterday."

"That's not true," Bev said, shaking her head. She turned to Bernie, and to her horror, he was twisting the ring and gazing at each person in the room.

"I saw it as well," Abigail said, with a firm nod. "Both butchers, in fact."

"They threatened me when I was last here," Estera added. "That's why I left so soon, sir."

Bev's frightened gaze landed on Dag, and her heart sank to her stomach as he took a step toward Vellora. "I see."

But to her utter surprise, the soldier walked up to *Bernie* and grabbed his left hand, inspecting the ring.

"You were right," Dag said to Bev. "This is magical. An empath ring."

"W-what?" Bernie took a step back, pulling helplessly at his hand stuck in Dag's firm grip. "You're mad. It's just a ruby ring."

The soldier flashed a knowing grin, showing off his iron bangle that somehow looked familiar to Bev. "Do you really think a magic hunter like me wouldn't be prepared? I felt your magic, sorcerer, and I blocked it."

"S-sorcerer?" Bernie laughed nervously. "I'm not a sorcerer, I'm just a traveling jack-of-trades, you know. Just in town. Found this in the inn. Hadn't a clue that it was magical." He looked at Wallace. "It's *his!*"

"I've never seen that thing before in my life," Wallace said, folding his arms across his chest. "Except on Bernie."

Beside him, Paul narrowed his gaze before nodding. "Me neither. It's certainly not my husband's."

"I last saw it on him, too," Collin said, catching Bev's gaze.

"You're all *lying!*" Bernie cried. "It's not mine!"

"Whether it's yours or not," Dag said. "I just witnessed *you* attempting to coerce a member of the queen's special service with magic. A very serious charge, indeed."

Bernie paled considerably.

"So does this mean I get to go home tomorrow?" Estera asked. "Since, you know, I'm the one who found it…?"

"I think the innkeeper found it," Flanigan replied dryly.

"Oh, no," Bev said, holding up her hands. "It was all Estera. She's the mastermind who was investigating Bernie. That's why she left and came back, after all. She was…trying to find out who was sending the Witzels these threatening letters. Followed them to Herman's house and overheard everything." Bev nodded at her. "You've got quite the mastermind on your hands, Mr. Flanigan. She deserves a medal."

Estera's mouth fell open, but she didn't argue, watching her boss with bated breath.

"I suppose. But you'll have to meet up with us in three days," he said. "In Sheepsburg. I have a lead on a dragon shifter I need to investigate." He adjusted his cloak. "Now if we're all finished here, I'd like to get *some* sleep tonight. Estera can keep watch over the prisoner she so *keenly* identified."

"Wait, I have gold!" Bernie cried. "I can—"

"Right, that." Ida marched across the room and plucked the satchel off Bernie's hip. "I'll be taking that back, thank you."

"Wait a second," Abigail said, holding up her hands. "There's still the matter of the registration card. Is it missing or not completed or what?"

"Oh, it's right here." Vellora reached into Bernie's pocket and plucked out two cards. She discarded one, presumably the blank one, and marched the other over to Abigail.

The registrar read the form three or four times before nodding. "This looks to be all in order."

"I wouldn't do *anything* to jeopardize my family's safety," Vellora said earnestly. "I promise you. Ida means everything to me."

Abigail flashed her a nervous, but genuine smile. "I can understand that. Dag? Take him away."

Flanigan looked irked to be ordered around by a registrar, but did as instructed anyway, with Estera, Abigail, and Collin following behind.

"*Magic* ring?" Paul asked, turning on his husband. "Wallace, seriously—"

"It was Bernie's. I think we all heard that, right?" Wallace said, chuckling nervously. "I wouldn't be caught dead being so irresponsible. Wielding magic when there's magic hunters all over this country. Surely, you know I'm much smarter than that, right?"

Paul gave his husband a dirty look as they walked across the street together, leaving Bev and the butchers alone.

"I guess we can afford to throw our solstice party after all," Ida said with a relieved laugh. She handed the satchel to Bev with a teary smile. "Assuming you're still up for it after all this chaos?"

Bev pushed the gold back into Ida's hand. "For you two, it's on the house."

CHAPTER TWENTY~TWO

The next morning dawned warm—warmer than it'd been in days. Flanigan and the other five soldiers took off with Bernie before dawn, and Bev hadn't been happier to see the back end of a guest since Karolina and her crew left Pigsend. Estera, positively giddy with joy at being able to go home, left shortly after.

The timing couldn't have been better, because Wim's solstice cooking schedule demanded an early start. She began with the rosemary bread, and as she finished that, Ida arrived with the first cuts of meat for the oven.

"Are you two all right?" Bev asked.

"Well, Vellora had some words with me about hoarding gold," Ida said, rubbing the back of her neck. "But we… we had a good talk last night. I mean, we had a *lot* of meat to carve up, so we were awake anyway. But…" She sighed. "She told me about the battle, about her home, her family. I never want to see that Bernie fellow again, but in some ways, Vel and I are closer than ever."

Bev smiled. "I'm glad to hear that."

"And Vel says that she doesn't want to go back to her village, she wouldn't mind taking a vacation to the south. A warm beach, she says." Ida shrugged. "Assuming the town will survive without its butchers for a while."

"I'm sure we'll manage," Bev said, walking to a simmering pot on the stove and lifting the lid to stir her wassail. "You two deserve a break."

Ida inhaled. "What's in that? Cloves? Cinnamon?"

"A little ginger, too, courtesy of Allen," Bev said, checking the fire beneath the stove. "Can you check Wim's list for me? What's next?"

Ida leaned over the paper on the counter. "Seven o'clock, time to make a cuppa and kick your feet up."

"Har har." Bev wiped her hands on her apron. "What does it actually say?"

Ida grinned, and Bev was happy to see her free

of worry and tension. "It says you've got to get the loin marinating in some wine and spices next. But Vel is still working on the loin, so cuppa and kick our feet up it is."

"Unfortunately, I've got to get out to the front room to check on the guests. I'm sure some of them will be on their way." She put her hand on Ida's shoulder. "But you are, of course, welcome to put your feet up. I daresay you've earned it after the week you've had."

"Bev? Are you in the kitchen?"

Allen had arrived with his pastries. Bev and Ida met him in the front room, and Ida let out a squeal of delight as he revealed his confections for the morning: gingerbread cookies decorated with colored icing.

"Ida! Bev! Happy solstice!" he chirped, putting the basket down. "Bev, I wanted you to be the first to taste these and let me know what you think. Ida, of course, you're welcome to them as well."

"You've made so many," Ida said with a gasp. "Will you have enough for the party tonight?"

"The snow melted enough that my merchant could make it into town," Allen said with a smile. "Replenished my sugar and spice supply, so I've got more than I'll need for the winter. Besides that, I don't think there's a better occasion for making sweets." He beamed. "Say, Ida...would you mind terribly if I invited Vicky to the party tonight?" He glanced between the two of them. "It is...still happening, right?"

"Of course." Ida lifted a cookie to her lips and looked at Bev. "Okay, Bev, with me. One, two..."

Bev sank her teeth into the crispy cookie, getting a pungent taste of ginger, spice, and sweet icing. "Oh, Allen. This is... These are perfect."

"Do you really think so?" he asked, holding his hands. "I used mom's recipe, but...well, you know... I'm still a bit nervous using her recipes without any...um...assistance."

Magic.

"They're perfect," Ida said, wiping a tear from her eye. "This...Allen, I needed a cookie this morning. You've made my entire day."

He beamed.

"Cookies?" The Werst family had appeared at the top of the stairs, ready to travel. Peter came barreling down the stairs at the sight of the sweets, followed closely by his brother.

"Only if Bev says it's all right," Abigail said, offering a kind smile to Ida. "Good morning, Ida. I hope...well, I hope you slept well. All is...um... resolved, right?"

Bev nodded, offering the basket to the boys, who took two each. "Are you going to make another attempt at leaving?"

"It looks pretty good out there," Abigail said. "And if we leave now, we'll make my parents' house after dark, but we'll make it. I hope we can get the wagon out of the ditch."

"Oh no," Ida said with a frown. "Your wagon's in a ditch? Do you need help getting it out?"

Abigail nodded, rubbing the back of her head. "I was a dunce and wanted to leave before the snow had really melted, so... Well, it's near Ramone's house."

"Ida, why don't you grab Vellora, and we can see about pulling it out?" Bev said.

"We don't need—" Ida began, but Bev *and* Allen cleared their throats to quiet her. Her tawny cheeks darkened, and she gave them a bashful smile. "Let me get my wife. It's the least we can do after what you did for us yesterday."

~

Vellora, of course, had no qualms about helping the registrar's family, and the group (minus Allen, who'd needed to return to the bakery to work on the rest of his cakes and cookies for the evening) headed toward Ramone's house. To their surprise, the sculptor and Horst had already removed the wagon and were in the process of hooking up the horse.

"Oh, drat," Ramone said dramatically. "We were going to bring it to the inn to surprise you this morning."

"The roads are quite clear now," Horst said, patting the horse on the nose gently. "I think you'll be able to make it."

"Oh, thank you, *thank you*," Abigail said, tears streaming down her face as she launched herself at the two siblings. "You've been so wonderful. This whole town… We can't thank you enough for all you've done for us."

"Likewise," Vellora said with a nod.

Abigail turned to her, wiping her cheeks and putting on a serious face. "I promise you, I will conduct a *full* investigation of that…*scoundrel*. We'll make it right with all those he's taken money from, and make sure it doesn't happen again—anywhere!"

Bev glanced at the others and was pleased she wasn't the only one who thought Abigail might be a bit *too* optimistic about her ability to affect change at that level. But the villain had been stopped, and the butchers were safe, which was what really mattered.

"Oh, uh… well, thanks." Vellora's pale face had gone bright red as the other woman squeezed her hands.

"I take my job very seriously," Abigail said, straightening and adjusting the sleeping baby strapped to her front. "And I'm horrified that anyone would even think of besmirching our—"

"Okay, honey," Byron said. "I think she gets the picture. You're making her uncomfortable."

"Well, I hope you have a lovely solstice," Abigail said, glancing at the blue sky and warm sun. "It looks like the weather has decided to cooperate."

"Thank you," Ida said, nudging her wife out of the way to shake Abigail's hand. "Safe travels to you and your adorable family."

Bev helped Byron hook up their horse and placed a bag of biscuits and pastries—courtesy of Allen—next to the boys, who were happily seated under some extra blankets Bev had donated to the cause.

"You boys don't eat all this before you reach Middleburg, you hear?" Bev said with a mock glare.

"Yes, ma'am!" they said in unison.

"Thank you for everything, Bev," Byron said. "Maybe we'll come back to visit Pigsend in the summer."

"Yes, when there's no snow on the ground. At all." Abigail shivered. "All right, we've said our goodbyes. If we don't leave now, we won't make it."

They set off, and Bev waved goodbye, hoping that they'd make it to Abigail's parents' house before too late.

"Oh, goodness, I've got to get back to the inn," Bev said with a jolt, as she noticed the sun's position. "Ida—"

"Pork loin for marinating and shanks for the oven in an hour," she recited from memory with a small wave as she put her arm around Vellora's midsection. "We'll be by soon with all the meat needed."

"That all sounds delicious," Ramone said, rubbing their hands together. "May we attend?"

"Of course," Ida said with a wave. "The more the merrier."

By the time Bev returned to the inn, Collin, Wallace, and Paul were downstairs, helping themselves to tea and cookies.

"So glad we caught you," Paul said with an actual *genuine* smile. "I think the roads are passable enough that we'll be headed to Kaiser Tuckey's."

"They are," Bev said with a nod. "Thank you for everything. I'm sorry your ring was an unfortunate casualty of…well…"

"Suppose it's for the best that it wasn't with me," Wallace said with an affable chuckle. "You know, if I'd been wearing it, perhaps I'd be the one in chains right now."

Paul snorted. "Good riddance to that horrid thing. You don't need it. You're an excellent cleric without it."

Wallace turned to his husband, a bashful, surprised smile growing on his lips. "Well, thank you, Paul. That's quite a nice thing to say about your husband."

Paul slipped his arm through his husband's and beamed. "You deserve it every so often."

"Well, I, for one, am staying put," Collin said with a loud clearing of his throat. "Bernie's gold was as good as Kaiser Tuckey's, and I even got a nice bonus from the butchers if I agreed to stay and play their party tonight."

"That's wonderful, Collin," Bev said, hoping for everyone's sake that Etheldra didn't show up. "But unfortunately, the price—"

The bard handed her two gold coins with a wink. "Understood. And appreciate all you've done for me." To Bev's quizzical expression, he smiled wider. "The butchers also paid me an extra five gold coins if I'd help them finish decorating the front room for the party. So I'm quite flush at the moment."

"Just don't spend…" Bev began but waved her hand. "Never mind."

⁓

Wim's schedule was, as predicted, perfect, and by the time the front room began filling up with farmers, everything was ready. Bev had been so busy in the kitchen that she hadn't had a chance to see what Ida, Vellora, and Collin had done with the front room, but as she brought the first bowls of nuts and winter berries out from the kitchen, she gasped in surprise.

Ida had hung holly, mistletoe, and spruce from nearly every space in the room. In the fireplace, a large log was starting to burn, also covered in spruce leaves and other decorations. There were beautiful red doilies on each of the round tables, and Ida had added red ribbons to the backs of each chair.

"Where did the doilies come from?" Bev asked.

"Merv," Ida replied with a wink. "I made a quick trip out to see him before all the snow fell."

That certainly explained why Biscuit was on his hindquarters, sniffing the tables as if they already held something delicious.

"Biscuit," Bev warned her laelaps. "No."

He withdrew and wilted to the floor.

"You'll get plenty to eat later," Bev said. "It's going to be a wild night."

And it was.

More than forty came through the door, but luckily, there was enough wassail (and regular ale), food, and pastries to satisfy everyone. Allen's ginger cake was a masterpiece, three layers of golden cake with white icing, and his shortbread and gingerbread cookies were gone before the clock struck nine. The party showed no signs of slowing down, with everyone overjoyed that the snow had melted.

Grant Klose made a brief appearance, as did Mayor Hendry, who didn't see the value in schmoozing with her own constituents. Sheriff Rustin was happy to hear that Dag Flanigan had moved on, but neither Bev nor the Witzels told him what had transpired.

Ida was the life of the party, dressed in a white lace dress and new brown boots. Her black, coiled hair was down, swinging wildly as she bounced from conversation to conversation. More than once, her bright smile shone toward Bev, who was so pleased that her dear friend had the party she'd been hoping for. Vellora, who was as quiet as her wife was outgoing, stayed in the corner and talked shop with farmers, but Bev noticed the way she watched her wife.

"Excellent party, Bev," Allen said, coming up with a cup of wassail. "I haven't seen you drink any yet, and it's about to run out."

Bev took the cup and had a small sip. She'd been tasting it all afternoon, of course, but to stand and drink it was…well, lovely. She had to agree with everyone else's assessment that it was, perhaps, one of the best things about the solstice.

"Your cookies were a hit," Bev said, nodding to the table that had once been filled with them. Now there was nothing left but crumbs. "I think you've got the hang of this baking thing." Vicky Hamblin was across the room. "Now when are you going to make things official with your best girl?"

He ducked his head, his cheeks reddening, and made some excuse as he walked away.

"Are you threatening the poor boy?" Vellora asked, walking up to Bev.

"Just by asking when he's going to pop the question," she said with a smile. "Are you enjoying the party?"

"Not nearly as much as Ida, but..." Vellora grinned. "We're grateful to you, Bev. None of this would've been possible without you."

"Oh—"

"Seriously." Vellora put down her glass and took Bev's hands. "You are... We'd be having a much different solstice had it not been for you." Her voice caught in her throat and her eyes became wet. "Thank you."

Bev had never seen Vellora look so emotional, and it gave her a little tickle in the back of her throat, too. "Well, I can't have the best butchers in Pigsend leaving. Who else is going to provide my daily meat order?"

Vellora didn't laugh. "Can I speak with you outside?"

Bev followed Vellora to the butchers' back yard, a frown on her face. "What's wrong?"

"I need you to know..." She cleared her throat. "I wasn't completely honest with you about everything."

"Oh, it's all forgiven and forgotten now. Bernie's gone, Dag's gone—"

"Yes, but I haven't been able to stop thinking about what Bernie said, and I feel like I need to tell *someone* or else..." She sighed. "I don't want to tell my wife. I'm afraid she'll see me as a monster."

"Ida said you two had talked."

"I didn't tell her everything about the Battle of Eriwall," Vellora said. "The things we did, the people we killed. Innocents. Children. It was a massacre. One of the last stands of the kingside soldiers, we were sent in with a horde of powerful wizards and other magical wielders to..."

The stench of blood, the feeling of magic zipping through her veins, and the simultaneous thrill and dread of impending battle swam in her mind. The wall of people before her stood ready to die, and she knew she'd have to kill them all. Yet, there was one wearing a bangle made of iron who was impervious to her magic.

Bangle of iron.

That's where she'd seen it before. That's where she'd seen Dag before.

She'd fought him in the Battle of Eriwall.

She'd been at the same battle as Vellora.

"...so it's no surprise *that's* the battle he

mentioned. The soldiers involved, we just—" Vellora seemed to notice Bev had dozed off for a second. "Bev? Was it too much for me to tell you this?"

"N-no," Bev said, with a nervous clearing of her throat. "No, of course not."

"You just look..." She tilted her head. "Never mind."

Bev forced herself to forget her own memory of that horrible battle, and her equally horrible part in it, as she forced a smile onto her face. "You should tell Ida. She wants to know. She loves you, no matter your past. I promise, she'll be forgiving."

Vellora smiled, her eyes once again filled with tears. "Thank you for listening, Bev. You're a true friend."

"Get back inside to your party," Bev said a little shakily. "Enjoy yourself and forget this messy business."

Vellora didn't need to be told twice, dipping back through the front door. But it took Bev another few minutes to be able to do the same.

Bev continues her adventures in

BEASTS AND BAKING

Weary Dragon Inn

BOOK FOUR

Acknowledgments

This book skirted over the finish line just days before the arrival of my son, and I have to say, writing 180,000 words during the course of the second and third trimesters was…uh, a challenge to say the least. But with 300 Kickstarter backers raising $12,000 to get all three books, it was important to at least get the book on paper before the baby arrived. And I'm so grateful to each of the folks who contributed to getting this book off the ground—not just in physical form, but eBook and audiobook as well.

Thank you to my husband, for continuing to believe in me and allowing me the space to get this book down, even after I was released from bedrest. I'm so grateful to have you in my corner, and our kids are so lucky to have you as their dad. As always, my appreciation goes out to the village of grandparents, aunts, and friends who step in to help out with the toddler when needed.

My thanks to Natasia and Luke at Stardust Book Services for the brilliant map, Robert Ardy for the brilliant cover, Danielle Fine, my editor, and my typo checker, Lisa.

Thanks also must be paid to the MI(L)F Discord group, without whom I wouldn't have been nearly as productive. A good writing group is essential to a writer's sanity, and sprinting with you guys was so much fun.

KICKSTARTER BACKERS

A heartfelt thank you to the Kickstarter backers who so generously supported the first three books in the series:

Aaron Frost, Aaron Jamieson, Abby Brew, Abigail Conner, Abra Roth, Adam Cole, Adam Kerstin, Adrianne Carley, AingealWroth, Alaska Momster, Alessandro Colombo, Alexandra Fluskey, Allison Torres, Alyssa Emmert, Amanda Gerdel, Amy Chadwick, André Laude, Andrew Kaplan, Andy, Anil Kadam, Ann Cofell, Anna, Anonymous, aoife & ryan, Archibald Nastyface Hethrenton, Aruhi, Ashley Matics, Ashley Stark, Becca Stillo, Becky B, Becky Carr, Becky James, Bethany Pratt, Bettina Pickett, Blake Strickland, Blumpsie, Boris Veytsman, Bree, Brett Werst, Brian Bauer, Bridget Horn, Bridgette Findley, Brock Miller, C. A. Maxwell, Caitlyn M Nye, Caitlyn Miller, Camilla Vavruch, Carlos Guerra, Carly Occhifinto, Catherine Sampson, CAVE321, Chase Sanders, Chelsea, Chris A McGee, Chris King, Chris Ward, Christa Rumage, Christa S. Rickard, Christian Holt, Christiana Laudie, Christine Crew, Clarissa Gosling, Cody L. Allen, Colin Letch, Conor, Cullen 'Towelman' Gilchrist, Dale A Russell, Danielle Perry, Dave and Rose Fonville, Dave Baughman, Dave Luxton, Dave Marchetti, David Haskins, David Holzborn, David Lewis, Day Leitao, Dead Fishie, DeeAnna, Dexter

Jacobs, Doris Wooding, Douglas & Nicole Williams, Drea Laj, Dustin Thatcher, E. Snelgrove, E.M. Middel, E.V. Everest, E.V. Green, Eddie Joo, Edward E., Elise Roberts, Elizabeth F, Elle Wilson, Ellen Pilcher, Emily Gibbs, Emma Cohan, Emma S, Erica Blumenthal, Erika Jo, Eva Ali, Felicia, Gary Olsen, GhostCat, Gina Lucas, Gina Points, Ginny L., Golinssohn, Grace Parsons, Greg Rice, Greg Tausch, Gretchen, Hana Correa, Hannah, Heather A. McBride, His & Hearse Press, Hollow Mask, Hollysbookadventure, Howard Blakeslee, Isabel Johnson, J R Forst, J Truscott, Jan Birch, Jan Dierker, Janelle Boys-Chen, Jean Sitkei, Jeffrey M. Johnson, Jennifer, Jennifer Brown, Jennifer Eaton, Jennifer Katsch, Jeremy S, Jesi Blair, Jessi Pike, Jessica Guyette, Jessica Stanton, Joe G, Joe Monson, Joel silvey, John Idlor, John Markley, Johnathan Detrick, Jolene Pierce, Jonathan Snavely, Josh Samples, Joshua, Julia Byers, KA Ramadorai, Kanyon Kiernan, Karen Fonville, Karen Low, Karen Scharff, Karen Tankersley, Karley Rech, Kat Brady, Kat James, Kate Ehrenholm, Katie, Katie L. Carroll, Katie VanWyhe, Katrina Drake, Kaycee Castleman, Keelyn Wright, Keli, Kelsey Hunt, Kenneth Brown, Kiera Storch, Kourtney & William Stauffer, Krissy Pallen, Kristen & Eric Terlep, Kristian Handberg, Kristin Paine Wallin, KRR Lockhaven, Krysti Matheson, Kurt Beyerl, Lacey Holloway, Larry Couch, Laura L Nelson, Lauren Kildea, Leslie Twitchell, Lindachelle, Lindsey Ferebee, Lindsey Thurman, Lisa Henson, Liz Jordan, Lorin Jones, Luke Italiano, M. H. Woodscourt, Marc D Long, Marcus U, Marilyn Donahue, Marine Lesne, Mark T. Eckstein, Marte Myrvold, Matthian, MC, Meghan

DiMarco, Melanie Pokroy, Melissa, Melissa C, Michael B
Mitchell, Michael J. Sullivan, author, Michał Kabza,
Michelle E. LaCrosse, Molly J Stanton, Nathaniel Webb,
Nicole wagner, Niels-Peter, Nikita Johnson, None,
Noreen Gwilliam, Oliver Gross, OwainB, Patricia Miller,
Patrick Moore, Paul, peter jockel, Phil Beneker, pjk,
Polina "Polinchka" Bazlova, prefer not to be named :),
R.J. Marchetti, Rachel S., Rachel Stoddard, Rafi Spitzer,
Ramón Terrell, Raphael Bressel, Ray Lorenz, Raymond
B, Rebecca, Rebecca Buchanan, René Schultze, Renee,
Richard Deltoro, Richard Novak, Richard Sayer, Risa
Scranton, Rob Steinberger, Robert K. Barbour, Robert
Sanders, Robert Stuart, Roman Pauer, Rowan Stone,
Russell Ventimeglia, Ryan C., Ryan Scott James,
Samantha Eckiss, Samantha Landstrom, Sandy Garza,
Sarah, Sarah B, Sarah L. Stevenson, Scantrontb, Scott
Casey, Scott Walker, Sean Bradley, Sebastian Ernst, Señor
Neo, Serena M, Seth Alexander, Shadowfall, Shaelei,
Sierra Davenport, Sissel K. H. Rasmussen, sonoghen,
Sophia, Stefke Leuhery, Stephanie Bailey, Stephanie
Horn, Stephanie Webb, Stephany, Stephen, Stephen
Kotowych, Steve Locke, Steve Untch, Susan Buescher,
Suzann P, Taylor Winsor, Terri Connor, Terry, Terry
Evans, Momma, Tessa, TF Drifter, The Calderon-Medina
family, The Creative Fund by BackerKit, The Freeman
Family, Theresa Snyder, Tom Dean, Tony, Tracy Popey, V
G Murray, Valerie Bolster, William J. Robbins, Wineke
Sloos, xellos, Yngve J. K. Hestem, Zero

Also By the Author

The Princess Vigilante Series

Brynna has been protecting her kingdom as a masked vigilante until one night, she's captured by the king's guards. Instead of arresting her, the captain tells her that her father and brother have been assassinated and she must hang up her mask and become queen.

The Princess Vigilante series is a four-book young adult epic fantasy series, perfect for fans of Throne of Glass and Graceling.

The Seod Croí Chronicles

After her father's murder, princess Ayla is set to take the throne — but to succeed, she needs the magical stone her evil stepmother stole. Fortunately, wizard apprentice Cade and knight Ward are both eager to win Ayla's favor.

A Quest of Blood and Stone is the first book in the *Seod Croí* chronicles and is available now in eBook, paperback, and hardcover.

Also By the Author

The Madion War Trilogy

He's a prince, she's a pilot, they're at war. But when they are marooned on a deserted island hundreds of miles from either nation, they must set aside their differences and work together if they want to survive.

The Madion War Trilogy is a fantasy romance available now in eBook, Paperback, and Hardcover.

empath

Lauren Dailey is in break-up hell, but if you ask her she's doing just great. She hears a mysterious voice promising an easy escape from her problems and finds herself in a brand new world where she has the power to feel what others are feeling. Just one problem—there's a dragon in the mountains that happens to eat Empaths. And it might be the source of the mysterious voice tempting her deeper into her own darkness.

Empath is a stand-alone fantasy that is available now in eBook, Paperback, and Hardcover.

About the Author

S. Usher Evans was born and raised in Pensacola, Florida. After a decade of fighting bureaucratic battles as an IT consultant in Washington, DC, she suffered a massive quarter-life-crisis. She found fighting dragons was more fun than writing policy, so she moved back to Pensacola to write books full-time. She currently resides there with her husband and kids, and frequently can be found plotting on the beach.

Visit S. Usher Evans online at:
http://www.susherevans.com/

9 781945 438660